NO ONE WHO ENTERS DROY WOOD EVER COMES BACK . . . ALIVE.

And the fog!

She had not noticed the mist creeping in. It had come stealthily, silently, across the wood. Gray tentacles of vapor curled around the trees, touching her with their cold, clammy outstretched fingers as if to ensnare her. *This is the land of the damned, and you shall not escape.*

Carol Embleton broke into a run, heedless of the thick mud. The trees around her became living things, slapping at her with low branches, reeds clutching at her bare ankles as if to drag her down into their evil mire. *Come join us for eternity in our stinking cold mud.*

Suddenly her flight was brought to an abrupt halt. She would have screamed her sheer terror aloud had not a cold wet hand clapped over her mouth and nostrils with asphyxiating force. Another arm encircled her body and lifted her up off the ground. And in that moment she gave in, surrendered to whatever Fate had ordained. . . .

Also by Guy N. Smith:

ENTOMBED

THE WOOD

Guy N. Smith

A DELL BOOK

Published by
Dell Publishing Co.,
a division of
The Bantam Doubleday Dell Publishing Group, Inc.
1 Dag Hammarskjold Plaza
New York, New York 10017

For Barry and Alice Stamp

This work was first published in Great Britain by New English Library

Dell ® TM 681510, Dell Publishing Co., Inc.

ISBN: 0-440-19753-8

Printed in the United States of America

First U.S.A. Printing

December 1987

10 9 8 7 6 5 4 3 2 1

OPM

THE WOOD

PROLOGUE

Bertie Hass closed his eyes, braced himself for the limb-wrenching jerk when his parachute billowed out, tried to will it to open. The cold night air rushed by him, tore at his heavy clothing. *It won't open, Bertie.* A jeering whisper inside his head. *You know it won't. Didn't that clairvoyant in Stuttgart tell you it would happen like this?*

Falling, faster and faster. And faster. Now he was preparing himself for the crunching impact when he hit the ground far below. He could see it in the faint moonlight reinforced by the flames from his crashed plane and the inferno of a city way beyond the horizon. The night was burning like hell itself, and there was only one place he was going. Down.

Mission accomplished, Herr Commandant, the city is destroyed, razed to the ground. Pride, overwhelming satisfaction. You always lost men on raids, it was inevitable. Soldiers, airmen were of necessity a dispensable commodity in war. Secretly, selfishly, you hoped it would not be your turn, always somebody else's.

Falling.

And then the cords jerked him, twisted him, tore at his arms as though they sought to rip them from his body, bore him some grudge for his loyalty to the Fatherland. He almost blacked out, had a blurred glimpse of Ingrid's face again. *Darkness and the torments of hell lie below you. Do you not see the flames?*

The night sky was a fiery glow now, so bright that he

could not shut it out even by closing his eyes. He felt the searing heat, heard the muffled explosions; bombs still going off, incessant ack-ack fire, the drone of heavy bombers, interspersed with the hornetlike whine of Spitfires.

But that was all behind him, ten, fifteen, even twenty miles away. His plane had come down, the crew still inside it except for himself. A sense of guilt, cowardice. No, it was every man for himself when you got hit, everybody accepted that. Try and bail out, take your chance.

He was floating now, drifting steadily on a downward course, a sense of euphoria overwhelming him. The bombing and gunfire were barely audible; perhaps he had come even farther than he had thought. Just a faint orange glow over the horizon. He glanced down again, saw a mass of shadows, some darker than others, a silvery sheen beyond that was undoubtedly the sea. He certainly had lost his bearings.

Darkness and the torments of hell lie below you.

Bertie Hass tried to shrug off his uneasiness, attempted to shut out the voice that undoubtedly belonged to Ingrid the clairvoyant. He had not visited her only to learn his destiny; he had gone for other, more interesting reasons. Like the other Luftwaffe pilots who had introduced him to her. No more than thirty, long blond hair and a shapely figure which you glimpsed through those near-transparent garments she always wore, her fortune-telling was just a blind. The tiny crystal ball in the front window of her dowdy house signified other things than glimpses into the future. Not that Bertie had any proof of that personally; perhaps you had to be a regular customer with several visits behind you before Ingrid Bramer took you through into the other room. She had warned him not to go on this raid. Perhaps that was an invitation to stay behind and visit her again. It would have meant going sick, convincingly. There were ways, but Bertie Hass had never done anything like that in his life. You had a duty to the Führer.

He was much lower now, could make out silhouetted details of the land beneath him. A wood, a big one bordering on a coastal marsh. His mouth went dry. He might get caught up, break a leg, worse. If only he could make it to the marsh; a concerted futile effort, treading air with his legs, trying to propel himself along but all the time drifting lower. And lower. There was no doubt in his mind that he would hit the wood.

The trees seemed to move, long thick branches outstretched like weird arms trying to catch him. Lifting up his legs, dodging them, foliage rustling against the soles of his heavy flying boots.

And then he was down. A soft squelching thud on boggy ground, his fall broken by spongy marsh grass, the mud beneath it gurgling and sucking. For a few moments Bertie Hass thought that he had made it to the marsh, had somehow overshot the wood. He lay there in the darkness, then fought to extricate his legs from the boggy ground, saw that he was surrounded by tall trees, macabre caricatures with boles twisted into leering faces, lichen old men's beards. Hissing . . . it was the muddy water stirring and settling again. A patch of wan moonlight defied the deep shadows, showed him everything he wanted to see and a lot of things he didn't.

Miraculously he had landed in some kind of clearing, had barely jarred his body on impact with the ground. The big wood, somewhere to hide. Safety. He shuddered, a sudden pang of fear for no accountable reason. That smell . . . not just the stagnant stench of foul water. Something else . . . something *evil!*

Quickly, expertly, he freed himself of his parachute, and began splashing his way out of this tract of bog, leaving a bubbling protesting trail of disturbed mud in his wake. He grabbed at an overhanging branch, hauled himself up onto a patch of solid ground. The shadows seemed to have spread, enveloping him in a black shroud as though claiming him for their own.

He was aware that he was trembling, hated himself for it. Was not he a member of the select Luftwaffe, one of the Führer's chosen bomber pilots to whom fear was unknown? This place was the same as any other, just somewhere to hide until he worked out a plan to get himself back to the Fatherland. The mission had been successful and he was alive; it was his duty to return as soon as possible. The war would not last long now, France had fallen and Britain was on her knees. The hour of glory was nigh.

He found himself listening intently. No longer could he hear the familiar sounds of battle and neither was the sky still aglow with the fires of destruction. Bertie Hass might as well have parachuted down into some country where war was unknown, just the unbroken silence of a land at peace. It was decidedly uncanny.

The mud was oozing and bubbling, settling back down beneath the thick grass. A night bird called softly somewhere. He must remain here until daylight, when he would try to get his bearings. After that it would be a question of traveling by night, hiding by day, until he found an aerodrome. Stealth, combined with a little bit of luck, was all he needed. A plane, any plane. And once he got behind the controls they could not stop him.

He tried to dispel his feeling of unease but it would not go away. He was all alone in a strange land. An enemy, a beast of the chase.

A sound; like a foot sinking into deep mud, remaining there because to have extricated it would have made too much noise. Which all added up to stealth—to being *watched*.

Shivers up his spine, goose-pimpling his flesh all the way up into his scalp. Trembling fingers eased the push-stud of his leather holster open, drew out the heavy Luger automatic. Show yourself, pig, and you die. You are facing one of the Führer's Luftwaffe.

Silence. Even the nightbird was not calling anymore, just the almost inaudible sound of trapped gases escaping from the bog. But Bertie Hass knew without any doubt that there was somebody out there watching him.

Victor Amery had been up on the knoll since dusk. Three nights a week he was assigned to his post throughout the hours of darkness, reclining in a deckchair which he kept up there to make the long boring nights a little more bearable. Fire-watching, it was termed, and somehow you had to try and convince yourself that you were doing your bit for your country. That was what the Home Guard was all about, a psychological boost both for the able who were too old for active service and the population of a virtually unprepared nation.

"Caught with our bleedin' trousers down," was Victor's favorite phrase most nights in the Dun Cow before he went on duty. "Everybody could see it comin' but they kept on sayin' 'peace in our time' until bloody war broke out. Then 'who would've thought it?' So the best they can do is arm all the old fogies with twelve-bores and say 'give it the Hun good and proper up his arse if he dares to come.'" And he had come, all right, Victor reflected grimly. At fifty life was becoming very tiresome. A clerk by day and a fire-watcher by night. When the bloody hell did they think you were going to sleep? Fire-watching, that was a bleedin' laugh.

Until tonight. Jesus Christ, he'd watched some fires, like a gigantic Guy Fawkes Night and still going on. The Jerries came in drove after drove, the entire Luftwaffe, surely, concentrated on one target. The railway network first, roads and bridges, then they just let all fuck loose on the city. Victor saw the munitions factory go up, there was no mistaking it. Puny retaliatory fire, the Jerries were having a field day. But they got one, oh Christ, they got one big bugger! Good for our lads!

Vic saw the bomber coming his way, wondered what the hell they were up to. All the others turned back once they had jettisoned their loads. But this one was hit, losing height and then bursting into flames. Victor Amery saw it nosedive, explode in a field of cut hay and catch fire, burning debris everywhere setting the hay alight. Smoke billowed up, hung in the still atmosphere like those fogs that came in from the sea at times. Had you coughing, your eyes smarting.

Fire-watching.

And then he saw the parachutist out of the corner of his eye. At first he thought it was a bird, so big and graceful, but eventually made out the shape of a man, gliding. Heading toward the Droy Wood.

Victor cocked the hammers of his shotgun. A Boche, an enemy. A killer. Look what the bastards had done to the city, an inferno that was even now cremating its dead, hundreds, maybe thousands more trapped by the flames. He swung the gun to his shoulder, his forefinger brushing the trigger. Too far; three, maybe four hundred yards. Not even a WD-loaded SG would reach that distance. Regretfully he lowered his gun, narrowed his smarting eyes. The bastard was going to hit the wood all right, no doubt about that.

Victor Amery saw the parachutist clear a tall oak, then dip from sight, swallowed up by the dark shape that was the outline of Droy Wood. Rather you than me, mate. He shuddered, didn't want to think too much about the wood at night. There were too many stories, going back far too long. Half of 'em were probably fiction, village gossip. But there was no smoke without fire. He coughed, wiped his smarting eyes.

Then he was hurrying back toward the village, his shout ready for when he got within earshot.

"There's a Boche in the wood!"

The cordon was thrown around Droy Wood with an hour still to go to daylight, a makeshift village posse. A dozen Home Guard, some youths who were on the verge of being called up, and one or two old stagers who would act as lookouts. Twenty in all, a sparse force when one viewed the wood from the hills above, five hundred or so acres of swampy woodland. Patches of dense reed beds which had infiltrated from the adjacent marsh like stone-crop spreading from a garden rockery into a flowerbed. Trees that had died, rotted, but still stood firm. A very old wood indeed.

But it was when the fogs came in from the marsh that you had to worry, Victor Amery reflected grimly. There was no telling when they would come, winter or summer. A bright May day would cloud over, turn sultry, hazy; then before you knew it that vile opaque vapor was wisping up through the trees, blotting everything out. *And Jesus Christ help you if you were in Droy Wood when that happened!*

Dawn came, bringing with it clear skies, a glow that

could have been from the rising sun, or else a reflection from the city which still burned. You could smell the smoke.

A dog barked. Brutus, the Alsatian that belonged to Owen, the gamekeeper. Owen was somewhere abroad, nobody had heard from him for over two months, didn't bloody well want to, either. Like a lot of others you knew the next time you saw his name it would be on the War Memorial plaque in the church. Secretly, selfishly, you hoped so if you'd lost one of your cats in his snares or traps. That dog was a personification of its absent master; vicious. If anybody was in the wood, and in all probability the German was lying low there, he'd find the bugger. And if he didn't, then Tom Morris's Jack Russell would, a snappy little creature that raced and barked all over the place, sniffed every clump of grass in the hope of a scent; a bloody nuisance on any day except today.

Victor Amery could see the others spaced over half a mile in a half-moon formation. Waiting. Captain Cartwright and old Emson would be at the far end of the wood, the guns in a pheasant drive. Everybody else were the beaters. Take your time, tap every tree and bush with your stick. An assorted armory; twelve-bores, a couple of .410s, air-rifles, pitchforks, pick-ax handles, anything that could be used as a weapon.

A shrill whistle jerked Amery into action, had him moving forward with the rest of them, thumb resting on the hammer of his gun. That Jerry was undoubtedly armed, at bay. Nobody could blame you if you shot him. Self-defense; and think of all those folks who got caught in the raid last night. Women and kids. Anger: he would have walked with his shotgun cocked in readiness if the ground had not been so uneven.

Twenty yards from the wood. The dogs had already

gone in, the terrier yapping incessantly. Even with the dogs, Victor decided, it was like looking for the proverbial needle in the haystack. You needed a full pack of hounds, ten times the number of searchers, and even then the German had a good chance of holing up somewhere.

Amery's uneasiness grew once they were inside the wood. So dark, it was incredible how the summer foliage shut out the light, gave everywhere a kind of sinister green hue, the shade that film cameras exaggerated to produce an everglades effect. Everything smelled damp and rotten, the black soil wet, muddy. It had not dried out over the centuries. You got a sense of timelessness in here, even to the extent of being unsure whether it was day or night, kept glancing about you, expecting to see . . . you didn't know what you expected to see and that was what made it a thousand times worse. Childhood bogey fears came flooding back; if they were reality then this was their spawning ground.

Victor Amery stopped because Fred Ewart had stopped to light his foul-smelling pipe, the flare of the match almost dazzling in the gloom. By its light you saw his wizened features, the crop of blackheads which might have been taken for a dark stubble of beard except that his drooping mustache was iron gray. Pale blue eyes, alert, watching about him. Four-score years had not dulled his brain, only stooped the shoulders beneath the navy blue knee-length mac which he always wore, summer or winter.

The next man down was looking to Ewart too; he'd been around longer than most of them. Ewart glanced one way, met Amery's gaze.

"We'll no' find him." *We're wasting our time but I've come along just for the walk.* "They never find anybody in here. Remember Vallum? 1932. He killed his wife and her lover, ran in here, left a trail of blood where he'd slashed his wrists. A trail a child could follow but there was nothing at the end of it. It just petered out. Nothing. They won't find the German."

Victor Amery shivered. Damn Ewart and his tales of yesteryear. That was one of the reasons why Victor had almost stopped going to the Dun Cow. Night after night, it got on your nerves, stories you remembered when you put the light out. Always Droy Wood figured in them. Maybe he made them up. Yes, that was it, the silly old bugger took a delight in scaring folks. He was the source of the legends, told 'em over and over again till people believed them and passed them on. The wood was just like any other wood.

All lies. Fred Ewart's goddamned lies. But you never fully convinced yourself of that.

A shout went up farther down the line. They'd found the parachute. The terrier was yapping and the Alsatian was barking fiercely. Now the animals had a scent; the hunt was on.

Eager as the searchers were, somehow old Ewart dictated the pace as though he were in charge of the whole operation; a slow gait, his ash stick prodding the ground in front of him, forewarning him of soft squelchy patches. Flies swarmed, buzzing black clouds in search of human prey.

Victor Amery came upon the old house suddenly, paused in amazement, experienced a sense of revulsion. Once it had been a fine mansion set on firm ground in the middle of a wide clearing. Stately gables had crumbled, there were holes in the roof where slates had fallen and smashed. The glass had long gone from the windows and they frowned down like eyeless sockets, the broken doorway twisted into a snarl of malevolence. Go away, you have no business here!

Somebody had to check the interior. The party had bunched together, looking at one another, frightened glances, hanging back. Victor Amery almost cocked his gun, his thumb beginning to pull the hammer back. Not me, no, not me!

As though in response to some mute order they all went, five of them, Ewart in the lead, his ash stick tapping eerily, the strong smoke from his pipe wafting back at them, thick twist fumes that reminded them of a city not so very far away that still burned. And the dead whose flesh singed in the fire.

A ruin, nothing more. Stone floors where weeds struggled to sprout through the cracks, broken doors leading from one large room to another; all the same, empty and thick with the dust of ages, cobwebs strung between the beams, all the furniture long gone. Silence except for their hollow footsteps and the constant tapping of Ewart's stick. He was getting on all their nerves.

Upstairs, a precarious ascent, the timbers of the stairway groaning its protest at their weight and their intrusion. Bedrooms; just one single remaining item of furniture, a rusted iron bedstead. Once somebody had slept in it, maybe copulated upon it. It had seen birth, possibly death. Now its time had come and gone. It would remain here forever.

Nothing. An eager descent to the hallway, for once not waiting for the old man to lead the way back out into the clearing where hazy sunlight greeted them. Nobody spoke, there was nothing to say. We didn't find him. Nor we won't. There's probably a cellar. If there is we're not going back in. You can tell there's nobody in there—at least . . . not *alive*.

Fanning out into a ragged line once more, every one of them sensing the deepening depression among them, the futility of it all. He's not here, let's finish and be away from this godless place.

The dogs were silent, seemed to pick up the mood of their masters. It occurred to Victor that the animals had not followed them into the house, had skulked outside instead. Everybody was hurrying now, even Fred Ewart stumbling in his haste to keep up with them. *And what tales I'll have to tell in the safety of the Dun Cow snug. Because I saw what you didn't see.*

The smell was stronger now, a cloying putrefying stench that they tasted, had them spitting out saliva. Some of them recognized it only too well—the smell of death. In all probability it had wafted on the wind from the bloody carnage of last night's bombing.

Following tracks, forcing their way through clumps of reeds where there was no path, wary of bogs that gurgled hungrily when they inadvertently stepped into one. No longer searching, only wanting to be out of Droy Wood. If the German was in here then he would surely remain there. There's more than one person gone missing in the wood over the years. 1932. Oh Christ, shut up, damn you, save your stories for the Dun Cow.

Finally they emerged into daylight, a boggy reed bed that led up to the pastureland where Captain Cartwright and his companion awaited them, perched on shooting sticks with all the arrogance of landed gentry. Relief on every face, the terrier beginning to yelp and dash about excitedly again; old Ewart cutting up another plug of twist.

Victor Amery glanced up. At first he thought there was a thunderstorm threatening in the hazy sky, the sun a pale red ball that was fast becoming obscured. But no, they were not clouds which were drifting across from the marshes, rather fingers of white mist creeping over the land, spreading out, billowing. Hiding every landmark.

"That damned mist's coming in off the coast," Cartwright's voice was slightly unsteady, a kind of *Well, we've had it for today, chaps.* "Another hour and it'll be like a November fog. I guess the Boche has given us the slip. That damned wood's too big and thick. We'd need a whole army to search it properly."

"He'll no' trouble anybody again." Ewart's features were pale, his eyes gimlets that sent a chill through any who looked into them. "Nobody gets out of Droy Wood when the mist comes across. We were lucky, Captain."

The atmosphere had suddenly gone much colder. And now they smelled the stench of death even stronger than before.

ONE

It was a long time since Carol Embleton had last gone to a disco. She hated it, she didn't *have* to be here; she could have been back in her parents' small house on the edge of the village. Except that they would have asked questions and right now she was in no mood to answer anybody's questions.

Her anger showed in her expression, her actions, as she took up the fast beat, punched the air with vigor. Her auburn hair turned yellow, green, blue all in a matter of a minute as the colored lights flashed crazily; lit up her eyes, a savage scintillating red glow in tune with her fury. Then the colors faded, the bulbs dimmed and she was just a flitting shadow swaying venomously.

A bystander might have been forgiven for presuming in the half-darkness that she was overweight. Five foot eight inches, big-boned, but her waistline slimmed delicately between her full shapely breasts and her wide hips. Agile, twirling, challenging the beat to go even faster, her wide mouth compressed into a bloodless line of fury.

Damn Andy Dark! Yesterday she had loved him, today she hated him. She saw his features before her eyes, couldn't get them out of her mind; that was what being in love did to you. Handsome in a rugged kind of way, his long dark hair was thinning at the crown and he would be balding by the time he was thirty, but what the hell. Slim, always dressed in jeans and a rough plaid shirt, the binoculars strung around his neck as much a part of him as that sailor's beard which she had got to like so much after detesting it initially. A slow deceptive drawl that rarely altered. "Sorry I can't make it tonight, darling, but there's a team of naturalists coming all the way up from Sussex to film that colony of badgers I was telling you about the other day." You didn't tell me and even if you did I wasn't listening because I'm not bloody well interested. Most chaps of twenty-eight finish work at five and take their girlfriends out in the evening. *Girlfriend,* not fiancée, because I've taken the ring off and left it at home. I'll post it back to you tomorrow. I won't register it and if it gets lost in the post then that's *your* bloody hard luck!

Sweating, moving away a few paces in search of a vacant place. Those youths who had just come in from the pub were edging their way on to the floor and no way did she want to give them the impression that she was jiving with them. A lot of girls danced on their own, preferred it that way. Certainly tonight Carol Embleton wanted it that way.

She had made a big mistake, ought to have realized months ago that this was how it would be if you dated a nature conservancy officer. They were all married to their bloody wildlife, you were the "other woman." Sorry if I've come between you and your badgers, darling. Don't mind me, I'll stop at home and wait till you call me. I'll be a good girl, I won't even *look* at other men. Like hell; but she wasn't going to let those yobs pick her up. There *was* a limit.

Rocking all over the world. Legs apart, swinging her whole body from the waist upward from side to side, creating a sensation of dizziness as though your scalp might slip right off.

Maybe Andy hadn't taken her seriously. Well, he soon would when that ring arrived back. Posted tomorrow, first class, it might just get there on Wednesday. Not an idle threat made in the heat of anger; she meant it. This had happened just once too often. Andy didn't have to go filming badgers at night with these nuts. He was always on about people trespassing, disturbing the countryside, and if tramping through the woods at night with cameras and dazzling lights wasn't creating a disturbance . . .

. . . she winced as that red disco light hit her full in the face again, knew just how those poor badgers would feel . . . then she didn't know what disturbance was. Hypocritical. Okay, he was determined to go, and that was his decision. Likewise she made her decision. We're through, Andy, don't pester me, please. There are plenty of other girls, just like there are plenty of other chaps.

But not the yobbo breed. She moved her pitch again and just then the music changed, a slower record, smoochy. Romantic. That was fine if you were feeling romantic; if you weren't it grated.

She began to push her way off the floor, caught a glimpse of the clock at the far end of the hall. Eleven thirty. The disc jockey would be folding it in another half hour. If she walked steadily back home her folks would have gone to bed by the time she arrived. Christ, she couldn't face one of their inquests, their patronizing talk. "It's only a lover's tiff. You go and sleep on it and you'll feel altogether different in the morning. Andy's such a nice lad, you don't realize how lucky you are, Carol."

Maybe Andy was nice if you didn't mind sharing him with badgers and foxes and any other species which happened to attract his interest at the time. The cloakroom door was sticking and she had to force it with her shoulder. It had been like that ever since she had come to her first disco here when she was fourteen. The whole village was like that, didn't want to change anything, good or bad. Andy, too. He'd still be going out filming something or other at night when he was sixty. Which was a damned good reason for not marrying him.

The night was dry but cool as she shrugged on her sheepskin jacket, just a hint of autumn in the air. Horse chestnut leaves were already beginning to fill the gutters, they were always the first to fall. Andy had taught her that, damn him.

A sudden decision. She would walk home the long way, a circular detour following the B-road that went north and then skirted the Droy Estate. There was enough moon to see her way by and for sure then her parents would be in bed when she got home. And I won't feel any different in the morning, I'll make damned sure I don't.

She walked on through the deserted village, realized how it had suddenly lost its appeal for her. Twenty years she had lived here, hardly spent a night away except for boring old holidays with her parents and once she was sixteen she had stopped going with them any longer. She'd got into a rut, hadn't bothered with holidays at all. That was where she had made a big mistake. Then Andy (damn it, she couldn't get him out of her system, it was something that would take months) had come on the scene. A university education, traveled in Africa and the Middle East, all on a government handout to watch something or other in the wild which didn't want to be watched. And look what it had done to him!

Ragged clouds scudded across the face of a near full moon, the silvery ghostly light showing her glimpses of the surrounding countryside. Wild. Rolling slopes that eventually made steep hillsides, and further on still became mountains. Dark patches where forests grew, the terrain of the fox and the deer. And the badger.

Sod Andy Dark, this whole place reeked of him like he had made it with his own hands. She hadn't used to notice it much until she had started courting him. Now there was no getting away from it. Or was there?

Elizabeth, her schoolmate, had packed up and left the village when she was seventeen, gone down to London, found herself a job; *and* a feller, one who didn't know such a place as Droy existed. A sudden idea crossed Carol's mind. There was nothing to stop her from going tomorrow. London sounded exciting, she had only ever been there once, a day excursion by train while she was staying with Uncle Don and Auntie Ellen in the Potteries. London was a big place where you made your own life, didn't have it molded for you by a petty bird watcher. She had no ties, apart from her parents, and they would have to get used to life without her, give them something else to think about. She didn't have a job, had been on the dole since the trouser factory closed down. Most of the younger generation of Droy had shared the same fate. There wasn't much likelihood of finding employment so you just accepted your lot and found something to occupy your time. Now Andy didn't really have a *proper* job. Studying birds and animals in the hills wasn't *work,* it wasn't doing anything *useful.* It was about on a par with young Roy Bean, the Droy gamekeeper. He was worse, all he was bothered about was *killing* wildlife, setting traps and snares all over the place, firing his gun at anything that flew. It . . . damn it, it was starting to rain.

Cold rainspots gusted by the wind stung her face, had her turning up the collar of her sheepskin, wishing she had brought her umbrella. More than that, wishing that she had elected to go the short way home. It was too late now, to retrace her steps would make the journey even longer. And to make matters worse the moon was clouding over, leaving her with only a dim outline of the road ahead. So dark, in fact, that there was a possibility that she might walk right by the stile in the hedge up beyond Droy Wood and miss the shortcut across the fields to the village.

A hint of panic but she pushed it away. She wouldn't miss the stile, she had walked this way too many times, could almost tell it by the way the camber of the road sloped. A favorite stroll on a fine evening. With Andy. I wish he were here now. Liar, you don't, you never want to set eyes on him again. The bastard!

Autumn rain; sudden, heavy and cold, a hint that winter was not far away even though it was still only early October. Carol quickened her pace, felt her jeans beginning to dampen around the lower half of her legs. There was at least a mile and a half to go, she would be saturated by the time she got home. She hoped to God Mother hadn't decided to wait up for her. "Wherever have you been to get soaked like that, Carol, and where's Andy?" Oh shut up, Mother, I'm leaving home, going to live in London and nothing you or Dad can say will stop me.

And then she heard the car approaching from behind, coming from the direction of the village. It was still some way off, half a mile perhaps, the sound of its engine a drone like an angry insect.

Carol Embleton hesitated, turned to face in the opposite direction. Now she could see its headlights, twin white beams swinging over the tops of the hedgerows like the searchlights of an anti-aircraft gun searching the night sky for an enemy aircraft. She found herself stepping back into the undergrowth, remembered those teenagers who had come into the hall after closing time at the

Dun Cow. They had had too much to drink, wouldn't have passed a breathalyzer test; except that in Droy you didn't get breathalyzed, not unless you had driven crazily down the main street and bumped into a dozen parked cars. And even then it would depend upon PC Houliston being around.

It could be those yobbos. On the other hand it did not necessarily have to be. And as if to aid her decision the rain suddenly increased almost to thunderstorm force, a blinding downpour that had her stepping back on to the edge of the road. Catchy strains of that disco music came back to her, a "golden oldie" that the DJ had played, one that went back well before Carol Embleton's time.

"A thumb goes up, a thumb goes down . . . hitchin' a ride . . ."

The headlights dazzled her, had her averting her eyes, temporarily blinded. The tempo of the engine changed, slowing, braking, pulling up alongside her. She heard the passenger door click open. A Mini. The driver was leaning across, just an outline. Nobody else. It wasn't the yobs from the hall.

"Nasty night to be out for a stroll," a friendly voice, an accent that she could not quite place, certainly not the Droy border twang . . . "Or do you do this for exercise every night?"

"No." She found herself stooping, sliding into the empty passenger seat, glancing in the back as though she half expected to find those village louts hiding on the floor. But there was nobody. The upholstery smelled as though it had recently been polished, the kind of smell a meticulous car owner might take a pride in. A snug place on a wet autumn night. "I've been to the disco in the village. When I left it was a nice dry night and I felt like a good walk home. The long way round," she added and laughed. "That'll teach me a lesson."

"No boyfriend?" Joking, pushing the gear lever forward into first, gliding slowly away from the grass verge.

"Not tonight. We've had a tiff but I expect everything will be okay tomorrow." Now why the hell did I say that? It won't be okay tomorrow because I'm getting out of this place before I get involved again. 'Bye, Andy, your ring's in the post. *Your* ring, not mine.

Carol glanced at her companion, saw the profile of a man who was surely not much older than . . . Jeez, does Andy *have* to come into everything? He appeared to be wearing a suit but no tie, the wings of his shirt collar neatly turned over on to his lapels. A short, well-trimmed beard. No, not thinning at the crown, that would have been just too much to accept. He's not a bit like Andy and I don't want him to be. She almost said, "No, that's not quite right, everything won't be okay tomorrow because I don't ever want to see him again," but it would have sounded silly. You don't go around spilling out the intimate details of your love life to some stranger who comes driving along in the night.

"There's a stile in the roadside hedge about a mile further on up the road," she said. "If you drop me off there it's only a few minutes walk to my home."

"Fine." She thought he smiled at her but his features were bathed in shadow. "What's your name?"

"Carol. Carol Embleton."

"Mine's Jim. I'm heading north, I'll probably drive all through the night. It's nice to pick somebody up for a few minutes chat, breaks the monotony." He was dawdling at 25 mph, seemed reluctant to increase his speed. Carol put it down to him being grateful for a brief companionship. Even at 25 mph she was going to get home an awful lot quicker than walking. On their right she saw the start of Droy Wood in the glare of the headlights; twisted, stunted trees that seemed to reach out into the road with their gnarled boughs as though trying to halt lone travelers. She shuddered; that was one place she'd never been in, never wanted to go in. She could not ever remember Andy telling her that he had been in there. It was one of those damp depressing places you didn't go and not just because of the local legends.

"I was thinking of stopping for a few minutes just to smoke a cigarette." The speedometer needle had dropped to just below 20 mph now. "If you've got a minute or two to spare I'd be grateful for your company. It's going to be a long lonely night for me. I envy you your nice warm bed."

The hairs on the back of Carol Embleton's neck pricked and her stomach muscles seemed to contract. She caught her breath and when she spoke there was a slight quaver in her voice. "I . . . I'd rather not, if you don't mind. My folks will be sitting up waiting for me and my boyfriend could be round at our house waiting to try and . . . and make things up. (Liar.) Last time I went off on my own . . . he'd rung the police before midnight. It caused a lot of bother."

"We'll only be five minutes." He swung the wheel hard over, drove on to a kind of lay-by bordering the wood, a patch of rutted mud, chewed up by the tires of parked heavy vehicles where passing long-distance lorry drivers had been forced by their tachometers to take a break. A few courting couples perhaps from the village on occasions. But tonight it was empty.

"No . . . please . . ."

"We won't be a minute or two."

"I can walk from here, the stile's only a couple of hundred yards up the road." Carol fumbled for the door handle, felt a surge of panic, and then strong fingers closed over her wrist. Cold fear, she could not even manage a scream and she had not located the door release.

"I only want to talk." The stranger's soft tones would have been reassuring in any other place, any other situation, if his grip had not been twisting the flesh of her wrist with the ferocity of a Chinese burn. "You see, I don't get a chance to chat much, and when you're on the road most of the time, often driving by night and sleeping by day, you get lonely. You *need* to talk to somebody . . . else you'd go mad."

"Yes, I . . . suppose you would." She was pressing herself back against the door, wishing it would suddenly fly open and catapult her outside. Then she would run, and run. And run.

"How old are you?" He leaned closer to her and she smelled his breath, a sweet peppermint flavor as though he had been chewing gum recently.

"Twenty."

"And I'll bet you're not a virgin, eh?" A loaded, insistent question that anywhere else would have brought an angry retort from her lips. But not here.

"No . . . I'm not. But I'm not a sleeparound either."

"This boyfriend you've had a tiff with . . . he fucks you regularly?"

She turned her head away, didn't want to look into his eyes. It was probably a trick of the intermittent moonlight the way they seemed to glow, shine with a frightening lusting madness. "We have a . . . a relationship." There was a lump in her throat that was making speech difficult. She swallowed.

"He isn't the only guy who's screwed you, though, *is he?*"

"Look, I . . ."

"Answer me!" A hiss, a blast of peppermint-flavored breath hit her. "All I want you to do is to answer my questions."

"All right." Carol Embleton was trembling violently now, shaking with sheer terror. "No, I first had sex when I . . . I was just sixteen. A boy out of the village. Just the once, and I never had it again until I met Andy. Now that I've confessed, let me go!"

He was silent for a moment, reaching across her with his free hand, fumbling in the glove box in front of her until he found what he was looking for. She saw him withdraw what appeared to be a crumpled handkerchief, pressed it into her right hand. It was damp and warm.

"Do you know what that is?" His voice was barely audible now. "Go on, tell me. Have a guess if you don't know."

"It's . . . it's a man's handkerchief," she replied. Oh God, he was mad. If only Andy would suddenly come walking out of the trees. *We had to pack the filming up, too damned wet. Have to try again another night.* But Andy Dark didn't come, and he was not likely to.

"Dead right." A little giggle and then his tone reverted to that lusting whisper again. "But that isn't all . . . you see, I masturbated into it about ten minutes ago, just before I picked you up!"

The soggy handkerchief dropped from her fingers: revulsion and fear. Oh please God, no. You read about these guys in the papers every day, tell yourself they don't really exist and even if they do, you'll never meet up with one. And suddenly for Carol Embleton it was all stark, terrible reality.

"My name's James Foster." A chilling note of pride in his voice. "You may have read about me, seen my picture in the newspaper. You couldn't very well miss them. I raped a girl and the judge let me off. There was an outcry because the public don't understand, don't even try to. I raped another girl last week and now they're scouring the country for me. *You see, I killed her!"*

Carol felt her senses start to swim, almost fainted. She was all alone in a remote tract of countryside at the mercy of a sex killer who had dominated the media coverage lately. She remembered his picture on TV. It had to be him, even though it was dark and she couldn't see him properly. Oh, Merciful God!

"It was her own fault I killed her." Sadness, almost an apology. "I didn't want to, I really liked her. But she screamed and struggled, would have gone to the police if I'd let her go. Even now they'll have to go to a lot of trouble *proving* it was me. You won't tell them, will you?" Pleading, playing with her. "The feeling came on me real strong a short time ago," he continued, "so I pulled off the road and wanked. But it didn't do any good, didn't give me any pleasure, and I knew I'd have to find a girl. I couldn't believe it when I saw somebody as pretty as you standing there. Tell me, do you masturbate or does this boyfriend of yours satisfy you so that you don't need to?"

"Sometimes." Tell him the truth, you've got nothing to lose. "Not as much since I've been going with Andy as I used to in my teens. Everybody does it at some time, though, it's nothing to be ashamed of."

"See what just talking to you has done to me." He moved her hand downward and she tensed, almost snatched it away as she felt the rigid protrusion inside his trousers. He was opening her fingers out, guiding them in a slow rub up and down the stretched material. "I'll bet you've got a lovely little cunt . . . Carol."

Her heart was beating crazily. Any minute she would

panic, become hysterical, and that was how that girl had died earlier in the week. Calling on every vestige of cunning and guile, remembering an old worn-out joke some film actress was once supposed to have made—"When rape is inevitable, lie back and enjoy it." Carol Embleton certainly would not enjoy it but she was determined to cling on to life as long as possible. Oh Andy, I need you, darling.

"Okay, I'll let you"—she tried to play-act an enthusiastic feel at his erection—"but only if you promise to let me go afterward. Promise me that and I'll try and make it real good for you. Otherwise I'll scream and struggle and you'll end up by killing me. And then it won't be much of a screw, will it?"

"I promise." A schoolboy who has suddenly been promised an unexpected treat. "I'll let you go afterward, I promise."

She was shaking, fumbling at the fastener of her jeans, preferring to strip herself. That would make it easier. It isn't James Foster, that's just one of the stupid rape fantasies you used to have years ago. It's Andy, he's feeling you up, going to make passionate love to you. It's Andy . . . Andy . . . Andy . . .

It almost was Andy, he even lubricated her enough so that it didn't hurt when he penetrated her. But once they were coupled Andy disappeared and the lusting specter of James Foster was back again: stifling peppermint breath that almost suffocated her, wild thrustings as he bit her neck, squeezed her breasts until she cried out aloud, hoping he would mistake her shrieks for those of orgasmic ecstasy.

Make it good for him, it's your only chance of staying alive! He was bucking faster and faster on top of her, his eyes ablaze, his body lathered in sweat. Once his fingers caressed her neck; she nearly screamed but they dropped down to her breasts, began to twist and pinch.

An idea, a faint glimmer of hope because there was nothing else left to grasp at. She faked groans of delight hating him for every deep thrust, convulsing; somehow got him into a position where they sat facing each other. Then she went on top of him.

Oh Christ, it was awful, repulsive. She tried to close her mind to it. I have to do this if I'm to stay alive. Gyrating on top of him. You bastard, you've killed a girl but you're not going to kill *me*. Speeding up, she felt him going tense in every muscle, starting to shudder, on the verge of his climax.

And then came the moment she had been waiting for, the fierce shooting warmth of a male orgasm, his fingers grasping for her to pull her right down on to him. Her timing was perfection, coming off him in one fast movement, using her legs to power her backward, at the same time pressing down the door handle, using her weight to push it open.

James Foster grabbed for her, missed her. And then she was gone, bounding away naked into the darkness of a rain-soaked autumn night. Running blindly, taking advantage of those few seconds' start afforded her by the rapist's orgasm. Fifteen, maybe even thirty seconds' grace, the time span of a male ejaculation that would hold him there. After that he would come after her, determined to vent his terrible revenge on the girl who had spurned him, deserted him at the very peak of his lust.

Headlong flight, bumping into a tree, squelching in thick mud. Only after several minutes was she aware that she had blundered into Droy Wood, that she had panicked. Too late to retrace her steps, floundering on, stopping to listen. Oh God, what a fool I am! No, you stand a better chance in here: out there on the road he would run you down, overtake you; kill you! You have a chance here, in a thick wood with a thousand and one places in which to hide.

Listening, shivering with fear and cold. Silence at first then she heard him, splashing footsteps which had her pressing herself back against the bole of a huge alder. She had anticipated the sound of frantic rushing, one way then the other. Instead the watery footfalls were steady and deliberate, systematic, the slow approach of the big-game hunter who has followed his wounded prey into a dense swamp. Faint moonlight slanted in, broke up the dense patches of shadow, glistened on lying water.

Closer, coming this way. Oh, thank God he hadn't stopped to find a torch before setting out after her. She closed her eyes, an ostrich's futile hope that it would not be seen. If she had had some means of killing herself she would have done so there and then. Oh Andy, where are you, darling? I'm so sorry.

Her pursuer was only yards away now, his breathing labored. He paused. She cringed; surely he must spot her at any second.

But he did not appear to, wading on, cursing beneath his breath, talking incoherently to himself, dead branches snapping off, cracking loudly like pistol shots. Going on, deeper into the wood.

Carol Embleton scarcely dared to hope, told herself that he must find her soon. But the sounds of his search were becoming fainter and fainter until finally she could not hear him at all. Relief escalated into euphoria. She was alive, free; all she had to do was to retrace her steps back to the road, run until she came to the stile.

Hesitantly she stood up. The moon had clouded over again and it was raining hard, all about her were shadows, some darker than others. The road could not be far away, fifty yards, maybe less in a straight line . . . Panic threatened to engulf her again. That way, surely . . . which way? If only she could still hear her pursuer then she would know which way to go. But there was nothing but total silence.

It had to be *that* way, straight ahead of her, through that patch of mud. Fifty yards at the most.

Trying to move quietly, the ground cold and slimy, the rain driving into her face. Slipping, almost falling, but saving herself by grabbing a branch. It creaked alarmingly but did not snap. Anticipating firmer ground at every step but still her feet sank in, the bog gurgled, giving off a nauseating stench of stagnant water.

And still bog. Deeper in some parts so that she had to back off, try and find a way round. Perhaps it was bigger than she had imagined and on her headlong flight she had been fortunate in finding a reasonably firm crossing. This had to be the way, it *had* to. There couldn't be any other, the road was only a matter of yards away . . .

It wasn't. Thick mire, pools of water lying everywhere so that she splashed noisily. Listening constantly but there was no sound of the rapist. Off to the right, firmer ground here, resisting the temptation to run, looking up but the moon was blanketed by thick clouds.

And then she sank up to her ankles in another patch of oozing mud, almost screamed hysterically as she faced reality—she was wrong, *she was lost*! You can't possibly be. I am!

The rain was sheeting almost horizontally now, splattering loudly in the pools of water around her. Wading forward but having to give up because it was too deep here, striking off to the left but only meeting with another mire. One way, then another, biting her lower lip until it bled, sobbing so that she tasted salty blood.

Finally she blundered on to a grassy hummock, wet but firm ground, a spreading osier which had not yet lost its foliage sheltering her from the wind and driving rain. Sinking down, crying her hopelessness as she huddled her naked body into a ball. Cold, exhaustion, terror, all began to take their toll, sleep threatening to claim her.

I can't stay here. You'll have to, you don't have any choice. I'll die of pneumonia. Something a lot worse could happen to you if you go blundering about Droy Wood in the dark. You'll have to remain here until daylight.

Still listening. Sounds that were probably only the elements, the wind, the rain, dripping water. Shutting her eyes tightly in case she saw something in the blackness of this awful night.

Praying for daylight until eventually she fell asleep.

TWO

Andy Dark and his companions had abandoned their badger-watching project shortly after midnight. The creatures were reluctant to venture far from their sett on this wet, windy night. A couple had emerged, dispiritedly gone back inside again. A further wait of twenty minutes but no more had appeared.

"We're wasting our time," Andy had said. "They'll probably come out to feed at intervals throughout the night but no way are we going to get anything worth filming."

"Try again tomorrow then?" The tall man in the full-length thornproof coat was obviously reluctant to abandon the foray. "If we keep on trying each night, surely by the law of averages we're going to get something worthwhile sooner or later."

"You're welcome to come back tomorrow." Andy Dark's reply was abrupt. "I'm booked up every evening for the rest of the week, but I'm happy for you lot to keep on trying. On your own."

He was tense, uneasy. Angry, too. Carol had had enough of these nocturnal vigils and he couldn't really blame her. A conservancy officer was at the beck and call of not just the public but virtually every organization connected with wildlife and the environment. They wanted to see something so you had to go and show them. If it wasn't a success you kept on trying like Robert the Bruce's spider. You weren't expected to have any private life. You were everybody's twenty-four-hour-a-day servant.

"We'd prefer to stop on for a bit longer," the other said. "It seems a shame to throw the towel in just like that."

"All right." Andy nodded, sighed. "We'll give it another hour then."

In actual fact they had stayed another three hours. On a couple of occasions they had glimpsed a rather dejected badger coming out to feed and returning shortly afterward, but as a ciné-spectacular the night's operation had to be regarded as a failure.

It was 3:45 A.M. when Andy Dark parked the Land Rover in front of his small bungalow. Even as he switched off the engine he was aware of a telephone ringing somewhere, a muffled jangling, but you got the feeling that the caller was impatient, insistent, wouldn't ring off until you answered. At this time in the morning it had to be something pretty urgent.

Andy struggled to turn the key in the Yale lock. Damn it, he had been meaning to oil it for weeks, now having to use brute strength until it clicked open. The phone on the hall table shrieked at him, screamed its urgency. A sudden sense of foreboding had him holding back, not wanting to answer it because you only got bad news at this hour. Like that night the hospital phoned him to tell him that his father had died. For months afterward the echo of that call had plagued him in his sleep. Now he heard it again.

It required a sudden physical effort to lift the receiver, hold it to his ear. A half-whisper: "Hallo." No longer was it "Andy Dark. Chief Conservation Officer." Because I don't want to know.

"Andy?" A worried voice which he recognized instantly as belonging to Bill Embleton, Carol's father.

"Yes. What's the matter, Bill?"

"Where's Carol?" If you've got her there with you you're a dirty lecherous bastard but I hope you have because then she'll be safe at least.

"Carol? I haven't seen her tonight . . ." Andy Dark's voice trailed off and his whole stomach seemed to compress into a tight ball. A feeling that he might throw up. "I've been out . . . filming badgers . . . haven't seen Carol . . ."

Both men were suddenly silenced by their own fears, a terror which they knew they must share, couldn't bring themselves to put into words, a fleeting futile hope that it would go away.

"I'll be right round," Andy snapped, slammed the phone down and ran back out to the Land Rover. Trembling, fumbling, grating the gears. Oh Jesus Christ, please, she'll be all right. My fault, those fucking idiots demanding to film badgers . . . should have told 'em to fuck off or else left 'em to it.

Driving recklessly, swaying on the bends, the droplets of rain reflecting the headlights, showering water up on all sides. Alongside Droy Wood, a Mini parked on that lay-by. It didn't register with him, didn't mean anything. Right now he wasn't interested in anybody else.

On through the deserted village street, houses that might have been empty, everybody gone away. Nobody lived in Droy anymore, it was a place of the dead. Eerie. Braking, swinging into the small graveled drive of a long narrow black-and-white timbered cottage, the downstairs windows lit up.

Bill Embleton was waiting at the door, tall and gray-haired, scarlet braces holding up ill-fitting gray slacks, his features lined with anxiety.

"She . . . hasn't come home." His voice was cracked, a pathetic whisper. "Where in God's name can she have got to?"

"Don't let's start panicking yet." Andy pushed past him, nodded to Joan Embleton who appeared at the top of the stairs. "There's a dozen and one places she could be, quite safe. She was in a bit of a mood, you see, because I had to take out a party of badger-watchers tonight. We had a tiff, in fact."

"Oh, I see." Temporary relief on the other's face. "Then maybe she's just gone off somewhere. She might even be staying overnight at Thelma Brown's. They were big mates once." He glanced toward the telephone.

"Well, we can't very well ring at this time of night." Andy pulled a wry face. It would put all our minds at rest, though. "But I'll certainly check there first thing in the morning."

"She didn't act strangely at all." Joan Embleton descended a couple of steps. "I thought she was going out with you, though it's funny, come to think of it, you didn't come and pick her up. She'd just gone, wasn't in the house anymore."

"I'll get checking first thing in the morning." Andy Dark turned back toward the open door. There was nothing to be gained by staying here, putting forward all manner of theories. Carol had gone off in a huff, in all probability she was quite safe somewhere. A lot of girls did that sort of thing on the spur of the moment. "I'll ring you the moment I know anything."

A slower drive back to the bungalow, his mind still in a turmoil. Past Droy Wood, that Mini still parked there. Probably a courting couple. Andy envied them.

* * *

"But she was at the disco!" There was amazement on Thelma Brown's freckled features, still in the act of combing her long fair hair as she stood in the doorway of the semi-detached council house.

"At the disco!" Andy Dark's expression was one of sheer amazement. "That's absolutely incredible!" A sudden nagging fear had him asking, "Who was she with?"

"Nobody as far as I could see," Thelma replied. "I did think it was a bit strange myself, I must admit. I was with John, my boyfriend, otherwise I would have gone and talked to her. She was dancing all on her own, really seemed to be enjoying herself."

"When did she leave?"

"I couldn't be sure. John and I stopped on till the end and I know she wasn't there then because I looked for her when the lights went up. Good God, nothing's happened to her, has it?"

"I hope not." Andy felt momentarily faint, leaned up against the doorpost. "She might just be staying with somebody, I don't know."

"Maybe you should tell the police."

"I've got to check properly first, otherwise I could look a right fool." He smiled weakly. "I'll ask in the village first, see if anybody saw which way she went after the disco. After that, if nothing turns up . . ."

After that he didn't know, didn't even want to contemplate it. He just prayed that Carol would turn up safely and that everything would be all right.

The usual small village on an autumn morning, conventional housewives of the older generation brushing front steps, younger women walking their children to school. A routine that nobody wanted to change because it was an integral part of the life they knew, their very own tiny world.

"Mornin', Mr. Dark." An elderly lady with her hair tied up in a bright yellow duster paused, leaned on the stail of her broom. "I was only sayin' to our Bert this mornin' that we'd seen your young lady go walkin' by last night."

Andy stiffened. Here in Droy the villagers missed nothing, noted virtually everybody who passed their houses. Some even habitually kept a note of the registration of strange cars. A kind of hobby to relieve their boredom.

"You saw Carol?"

"Oh yes . . . but maybe I 'adn't ought to say. She weren't up to nothin', Mr. Dark, only just walkin' along on 'er own. I just 'appened to think it was a bit strange, that's all. None o' my business, though."

"Which way was she going?" Andy Dark's expression was grim, his eyes narrowed into twin slits. Inside he felt physically sick.

"Look, I don't want to get tittle-tattling." The woman was blushing now, embarrassed. "As I said, it's none o' my business and I don't want to get causin' any bother between you two. I just 'appened to mention it. Wish I 'adn't."

"Look." Andy's voice was terse, a sudden feeling of anger toward this woman who might suddenly go back inside and slam the door, "Carol Embleton is missing. Her folks are worried sick. I'm trying to find her."

"Oh!" Surprise, shock, twirling the broom head between her hands. "In that case . . . well I can't tell you much more'n I've already told you, Mr. Dark. She was walkin' quite fast, goin' *out* of the village which struck me as strange because if she 'ad been walkin' 'ome she would've turned down Thorn Street. So I said to my Bert, it looks like Miss Carol's goin' to walk all the way up to Mr. Dark's 'ouse. At that time o' night, too, and 'er 'avin' to go along by Droy Wood, if you know what I mean."

Along by Droy Wood . . .

Andy's stomach seemed to heave up and he tasted bile, stared straight in front of him, didn't see the street anymore, just a winding country road, the tarmac glinting black in the faint moonlight, tall straggling unkempt hedges on either side. And Droy Wood, dark and forbidding, that permanent smell of decaying vegetation wafting from it . . .

"Are you all right, Mr. Dark?"

"I'm fine," he lied, revved the engine of the Land Rover.

"If she didn't get to your 'ouse . . ."

"She probably changed her mind." He revved the Land Rover's engine even harder, engaged first gear. "Thank you for your help. I'm sure I'll find her okay."

He roared off, mentally cursed some unknown car owner for parking in the main street so that he had to pull in and wait for a slow-moving milk float to come by. Gripping the steering wheel as though it were his intention to snap it in half, following the snaking B-road out of Droy, eyes flicking from side to side, trying to inject some logic into the chance information which he had received. If Carol had walked this way then surely she was heading toward the bungalow. She knew he would be out so what was her reason? A make-up-and-be-friends-again mission? There hadn't been a note pushed through his door, he would have seen it if there had been. She could have cut back across the fields and gone home. She hadn't. Oh Christ Almighty!

Droy Wood loomed up ahead. That Mini was still parked there, nobody in sight. Perhaps it was an abandoned stolen vehicle. It might just have broken down.

On impulse he swung the wheel over, bumped across the rough ground and pulled up alongside it. Some clothing was strewn over the seats; a suit, a pair of jeans, a blouse top . . . *oh Jesus God!*

He leaped down from the Land Rover, frantically tugged open the door of the Mini. A crumpled white handkerchief fell out but he ignored it. Reaching inside, grabbing that pale blue blouse, almost afraid to look at it.

Carol's! It didn't have to be, they mass-manufactured these garments, you could buy them almost anywhere. A faint odor of musk. Carol always used musk. So did a lot of other girls. Trying to tell himself it wasn't hers, grasping at any reason why it should not be. Checking the bra, the red panties on the floor, those shoes . . .

And finally he had to accept that they all belonged to Carol Embleton.

Shock. A numbing wave that knocked him down on to his haunches, just staring at the interior of that car. The evidence lay before his eyes, he could not dispute it. Carol had been in this car, she had been stripped naked. Now she was gone but the car was still here.

And then his trained naturalist's eyes noted something in the mud. Footprints, naked ones. Scrambling on his hands and knees, a pioneer tracker reading the signs as one might read a book. Carol's smaller footmarks, partly obliterated in places by larger, heavier ones. *Heading toward Droy Wood!*

He walked forward a few paces, saw the marshy bed of grass and reeds that stretched along the perimeter of the wood, how some of the tall seedy stems were crushed flat, a muddy trail that led on toward the trees.

Andy Dark's brain was spinning. Carol and an unknown man had entered the wood, both of them walking; he hadn't killed her and dragged her in there to hide the body. Temporary relief. But *why?* You didn't go into a wet boggy place like Droy Wood to screw.

His mouth was dry, he felt himself trembling. This wood had a history of catastrophes, mysteries. All local rumors which he discounted, but nevertheless it wasn't a pleasant place, gave you the creeps just looking at it. Some of the bogs were dangerous, too. Only last year a couple of ewes had wandered in there and disappeared without trace and that was reality, not gossip.

Indecision. It would be cruel as well as pointless to alarm Bill and Joan Embleton at this stage. He could go back and tell PC Houliston but that would only result in the village constable returning with him to search for the girl, and the policeman would only be a hindrance; an old-fashioned village bobby on the point of retirement, slow-moving and phlegmatic.

There was only one thing to do and that was to go in there and look for Carol himself. Even so he pondered on the wisdom of his decision. Droy Wood was a big area, five hundred acres at least, a veritable wooded marsh choked by thick reed-beds on the coastal side. An army could hide in there and not be discovered. The old-stagers in the Dun Cow related how in the last war a Luftwaffe pilot had parachuted down in it and had never been found. In all probability he had sneaked out before the search party began scouring the wood on the following day, Andy had always maintained.

Nevertheless, the prospect was a daunting one. The nature conservancy officer glanced up at the sky. The heavy overnight rain had passed on, leaving in its wake a dull misty morning. It was drizzling slightly, and it had the look of one of those calm early autumn days that could just bring the first seasonal fog later on.

Beware Droy Wood when the mist comes in from the sea!

Andy shivered, struck off across the soft marshy ground, his eyes fixed on the trail of trampled reed stalks ahead of him. Fortunately he wore his habitual Wellington boots, for the water in places came up almost to the tops. One thought he tried to blank out of his mind, that of Carol Embleton floundering in this mire in the pitch darkness. It did not bear thinking about.

And if she was not still alive then he did not want to be the one to find her.

THREE

PC Jock Houliston chewed on the stem of his large bent pipe. He attempted to relight the wedge of soggy tobacco, gave it up as a bad job and stared disdainfully at the large-scale OS map which adorned the wall of his office. Suddenly life had ceased to be a pleasant run-in to retirement. He could have done without all this, Jesus Christ he could!

He was overweight and had an unhealthy ruddy complexion, a host of burst cheek veins giving it a purplish appearance. Balding, with rotund features, he prided himself in being the typical jovial policeman, the last of a dying species. Next year the inhabitants of Droy would have to put up with some young upstart from the town, who would be eager to show his authority in his first posting. That would be an end to the after-hours drinking sessions in the Dun Cow most nights. Which was one reason why Jock had decided to leave the area altogether. Let them remember him along with "the good old days." With a low sigh he turned back to face the sharp-featured CID man whose eyesight was apparently good enough for him to study the map from where he stood on the other side of the desk.

Detective-Sergeant Jim Fillery was small and insignificant at first glance. In the street you would pass him by, not even giving him a second glance, which was a considerable advantage where a plainclothes policeman was concerned. Short fair hair, the only distinctive feature about him was his eyes, pale blue chips of ice that gave you some insight into the man behind them. Vicious, a man not to be trifled with. Three years ago he had undergone a special inquiry; during an interrogation a prisoner charged with indecent assault on a seven-year-old child had seemingly fallen and cracked his skull on the wall of the interview room. There followed the usual public outcry against "police brutality."

But the Committee's findings had been that the prisoner had slipped and fallen during a struggle with Fillery, and that the policeman was in no way to blame. Six months later the injured man had died suddenly of a brain hemorrhage and there was a further storm of protest, the dead man's family demanding that the original inquiry be reopened. But they had lost their appeal and Fillery's reputation was established. The hard man of the force—but one day he would overstep the mark.

"We know for certain Foster's in this area." Fillery had a quiet voice but you listened extra hard because he wasn't the type of man to take kindly to constant requests to repeat what he had said. "That Mini by the wood is the one that was stolen in Stoke-on-Trent. I'm pretty certain that we won't find this Embleton girl alive although the Super would slay me for saying that. It beats me, though, what's happened to Dark. Maybe Foster has jumped him in the wood, killed him, although sex killers generally do not assault anybody except their chosen victims. Anyway, we'll find out today, I've no doubt, when we draw Droy Wood. The media are billing it as one of the most intensive manhunts of the decade."

"It'll need to be." Resentment in Houliston's voice. "Droy Wood is the nearest thing you'll find approaching the Everglades in this country!"

"We'll sort it out," the CID man snapped. "Every

available police officer from a twenty-mile radius, a whole company of army rookies who are damned glad to have something useful to do, plus some of the best tracker dogs in the force. We'll find the girl and Dark, and if Foster's in there he won't get away this time, I can assure you!"

There was a personal bitterness in Fillery's tone now. He remembered his last encounter with James Foster, that rainy November day when he had arrested him on a rape charge, two devastating physical blows delivered with such expertise to the abdomen that they had not left a single mark. Just another of thousands of sex perverts who ought to be castrated, a clear-cut case that should have put Foster away for a few years. Instead, that weak-minded judge had given him a suspended sentence with a recommendation for psychiatric treatment. The stupid senile old fucker! The next time Foster had killed, and now it looked like he had killed again. Fillery was going on that manhunt personally, he had a score to settle with James Foster; he wanted to be the one to find him crouching naked under a bush. Pleading for mercy which wouldn't be given; just ten seconds alone with him.

"There's a thick mist come in off the coast." Houliston's expression was stoic. "And in Droy Wood that's bad."

"I've heard all this crap about what happens when the mist covers Droy Wood." The detective laughed harshly. "The only thing it'll do will be to make our task that bit harder. But we'll thrash that wood out, every bloody reed and bush. If he's there, we'll get him, make no mistake about that."

Jock Houliston nodded. Vehicles had been arriving since shortly after daybreak, police cars and vans, army transport trucks, and, of course, the usual following of sightseers, ghouls who hoped to catch a glimpse of the sexually mutilated body. In many ways they were worse than the killer because their motives were the same, perverted lust, voyeuristic vultures preying on the carnage.

Suddenly Droy was in the eyes of the whole country.

The mist had come in overnight, had not melted with the dawn, a low-lying mass of white vapor that seemed to stop once it reached the coastal road. Eerie, even a casual bystander could not miss the implication; its task was to cover Droy Wood, protect the evil that lurked there. Cold and clammy, it had a damp cloying smell, the reek of rotting vegetation, a continual process that spanned centuries and would go on until the end of time.

Vehicles were parked along the road which bordered the wood. The Mini and the Conservancy Land Rover were still there, cordoned off with orange tape. Later they would be moved.

A uniformed police superintendent was talking to a bunch of young soldiers, frequently pointing with his baton across to where the big wood lay screened by the fog. Everybody must keep in sight of the next man in the line, a dog every fifty yards. A couple of insignificant police marksmen just in case. In all probability they wouldn't be needed. Every eventuality was catered for.

Police on the flanks with more Alsatians in case Foster made a run for it, which was a strong possibility. Search every reed-bed, every bush, take your time.

Jock Houliston pulled on his Wellington boots, did not like this one little bit. These boys did not understand what they were up against; it was impossible trying to tell them. They scorned the rumors because they did not understand. Jock had been a lad attending Droy school that time the German parachuted down. He remembered the search, listened to his father's own version of it. The Jerry was in there, no matter what anybody might say, and they would have found him if the mist had not rolled in. Just like it had today.

The search wasn't just a futile task, it was a dangerous one. Jock had spent some considerable time going through the missing-persons file. Somebody went missing somewhere every day, often folks who had a good reason for disappearing, just wanted to lose their identity and start a new life elsewhere. But the policeman had a very strong belief that a number of those in this area had found their way into Droy Wood. Some of the bogs were dangerous, they could suck you down without a trace and all that was left was your name on the missing-persons file for perpetuity.

He joined the line, moved a few yards farther up so that he could see the outline of the next man down, a young soldier. The constable's mouth was dry, he could taste the decay in the atmosphere; coughed and spat. On his right was Roy Bean, the Droy Estate's gamekeeper.

Somebody blew a whistle and they were off, slow measured strides, their footsteps muffled in the thick fog. A sort of movie sound effect for water buffalo tramping restlessly around a water hole.

Houliston checked his watch. 8:25. It was going to be a long day. Voices, shouting all the time, searchers keeping in touch with one another. Frequent stops. Once somebody blundered into a mire, had to be pulled out. A glimpse of a fleeting shape ahead of them, but the dogs did not seem to find a scent. They were quiet, almost subdued, unwilling to venture far ahead. You sensed the general atmosphere of reluctance. Of fear, too.

Jock knew that they had to come upon the old house soon. He had seen it once before, many years ago, but had never been inside. He recalled his father's story of that day they searched it for the Boche.

"You wouldn't have gone in there on your own, lad," old Mac Houliston had sucked his lips as though he didn't want to relate the story but thought he ought to in case his son might venture there sometime on some idiotic schoolboy prank. "There's nothing there except decay and filth and a rusty old iron bedstead, but all the time you got the feeling that there was somebody watching you. Spooky. We checked all the rooms then got out as quick as we could. I reckon there has to be a cellar but nobody wanted to hang around looking for it. If there is, then the Jerry could well have been hiding down there. *He might even still be there now, just a skeleton propped up in the corner where he fell asleep . . ."*

And that was one of the things worrying Jock Houliston today. That old ruin, if it still stood, it would have to be searched thoroughly, the cellar investigated.

"There's the house." The man closest to him had moved in and the constable saw that it was Roy Bean, the Droy gamekeeper. Angular features with protruding top teeth, yellowed with nicotine, hardly served to enhance his unfortunate looks. His left eye was set a shade lower than the right, his nose too small. Houliston had once heard a summer tourist remark rather tactlessly, "I suppose that's the fucking village idiot." Yet the young keeper always wore moleskin breeks tucked into polished gaiters, seemed to take a pride in the once-traditional dress of his profession. His own status symbol, his father's and grandfather's before him, and if people were too ignorant to notice the "uniform" of an honored profession then that was just too bad.

"Aye." Jock pushed his peaked cap on to the back of

his bald head. "The Droy House, what's left of it, at any rate."

Even the swirling fog could not hide the dereliction. The rafters had conceded finally to the perseverance of an army of woodworm and had collapsed, showering the slates down inside, smashing most of the upper story, splintering it right down to ground-floor level. A heap of debris; soon the remnants of the outer walls would crumble and that would be the end of the once-splendid home of the Droy family.

Others were converging on the clearing now, whistles being blown to halt the advancing line of searchers while the ruined building was investigated. Houliston groaned to himself as he spied Fillery. The CID man would make a meal of this lot; they could be here for hours.

"You come inside with me, Constable," the detective motioned to Houliston. "You wait here, keeper. I expect you know this place well, better than most of us here, but we'll call you if we need you." We don't like civilian involvement unless it's absolutely unavoidable.

"No, sir, I never come here." Bean's tone was one of uncertainty, reluctance. "We don't shoot the wood anymore. It ain't safe."

"Too many bogs, eh," Fillery cut in quickly. He didn't want this yokel to begin retelling the Droy legends. They were concerned with facts not rumors today. "You follow me, Constable, and we'll take a look inside. We'll have to tread carefully, we don't want the whole lot collapsing on top of us."

Somehow the girders still held the doorway open, the door itself long gone, a dark dusty square remaining. Threatening, defiant; almost an "abandon hope all ye who enter here," Houliston thought. But Fillery was moving forward with a cautious eagerness, peering inside, producing a torch and swinging its beam on the interior. "Let's go inside," he said.

The torchlight revealed walls covered with moss and lichen, condensation which streamed down the stonework and dripped steadily into puddles on the floor. Houliston swallowed; the sound reminded him of a radio play he used to listen to as a youngster, propping his bedroom door open at night so that he could hear the wireless in the living room downstairs. A headless body in an empty house, the steady drip-drip of blood from the landing to hallway. Ugh!

"Look!" Houliston jumped visibly as Fillery spoke, saw the CID man drop to his knees. "Now that is *very* interesting!"

The other checked the instinctive "what?" The detective force invariably adopted a superior attitude over the uniformed branch, a kind of Holmes and Watson relationship; surely you see what *I* see.

Jock Houliston leaned forward, peered intently at the floor. He saw slate chips and fragments, a mound of thick moss—*and clearly imprinted on the latter was a naked human footprint!* He felt his flesh go cold, start to creep, glanced back toward the doorway. Outside he could hear Roy Bean talking to some of the soldiers. Outside—it seemed a million miles away right now.

"It's fresh, too," Fillery breathed, "see how the impression has squelched right down into the spongy moss which hasn't sprung back into place yet. A matter of hours ago, I'd say. Look, there's another . . . and another. Going right on into the hallway!"

PC Houliston didn't want to follow his companion. Somebody was in here, there was no doubt about that. Fine, they were hunting a fugitive and that aspect did not worry him; if only it had been anywhere else except Droy

House! The old stories came flooding back. Tales recounted by his father of how a few generations ago the Droys were the cruel landowners of these lands, how they assisted the Customs officers in the apprehension of smugglers coming ashore on this deserted stretch of coast beyond the wood. Prisoners were taken, brought back here, some terrible tortures inflicted upon them. The villagers heard the screams in the dead of night and neither the smugglers nor their contraband were heard of again. Stories, fables. Fiction. You could tell yourself that any other place except here.

"Let's see where they go to." Fillery's voice echoed in the confined space as he moved forward, his torchbeam scanning every patch of shadow. Houliston followed; he didn't have any other choice. Oh God, why couldn't all this have waited another year?

"That must be the cellar." Suddenly the white beam was focused on what looked like an open trap door in the corner of the hallway. Even Jock Houliston did not need the sharp-eyed detective to show him the piles of rubble that had been cleared from it; more moss, more footmarks . . . going right on down into the bowels of Droy House. *"Whoever it is, they're down there, all right!"* Whispering now, the detective alert, his hand in the pocket of his raincoat. He was armed, he would shoot if he had to.

Descending a step at a time, shining the torch on ahead of him, leaving no niche in the ancient stonework unexplored. There was no debris down here, the cellar having been protected from structural collapse, just bare wet walls and an overpowering stench of damp staleness. And so very cold. You sensed the evil.

Houliston moved closer to the detective, didn't want to be left alone in this awful blackness. He prepared himself for the gruesome sight of the murdered girl; she just had to be down here. Maybe Dark, too. And Foster. The place was bigger than you would have thought, like ancient catacombs stretching on and on, the dripping roof supported by stone pillars. All manner of frightening thoughts came to plague the Droy policeman; suppose the roof collapsed with the vibrations of their movements, trapped them alive down here. Catalepsy. Childhood bogies emerging from the cupboard. You *do* believe in spooks. Can't you hear them whispering in the darkness, touching you with their cold clammy fingers?

"Christ on a bike!" Detective-Sergeant Fillery pulled up so suddenly that Houliston cannoned into him, clutched at him to save himself from falling.

They both stared, words were superfluous. In the torchlight they saw that they had reached the end wall of the cellar, built in a kind of bow, maybe eight feet high, some fifteen feet across.

And there fastened to the stonework was a series of rusted manacles, five or six pairs of them with matching leg irons a couple of feet from the floor beneath them. You saw in your mind the pain-wracked bodies of centuries ago, broken limbs threatening to jerk out of their sockets; heard their cries of torment. Oh Jesus, you wanted to slap your hands over your ears to try and shut out the pitiful wails, the screams of women and children. You smelled death, the stench would never leave this place, the evil here would never die.

"Well . . . there's nobody here." Houliston uttered the words, a hint that they should be leaving. Something inside you told you to run, get the hell out. But the sharp-eyed Fillery had spotted something else.

He was on his knees again, poking on the floor with a forefinger and holding it up to his nose, gingerly giving it a lick with his tongue. Then he straightened up, turned back to his uniformed colleague.

"Blood," he spoke in a whisper, "fresh blood!"

"Oh Lord." Houliston recoiled a pace.

"And more footprints." The detective's features were pale in the reflected glow from the torch. "All of 'em coming in here, stopping at this infernal wall . . . *but none going back out!*"

"That's . . . impossible!"

"Yes, if you look at it realistically, but it could be a trick though Christ alone knows what anybody would get out of setting up a thing like this. Undoubtedly this is an old torture chamber going back to the early eighteenth century. Not that that is going to figure in any way in our problem." Somehow the detective's voice did not ring true. He, too, was scared beneath the bluff façade he had created.

"Well, there's definitely nobody in the house," Fillery told the waiting group as they emerged into the foggy clearing. "The ground floor and the cellar are empty and the upper story has completely fallen through. Let's continue with the search outside."

PC Houliston checked his watch. 11:30. God, they must have been in that place almost an hour. In spite of this foul stinking mist it was a relief to be outside.

The line fanned out again, waited for the whistle to blow to send them forward again. If anything the fog was thicker, creating weird unearthly shapes out of the twisted marsh trees, boughs that became arms making threatening gestures at these intruders; the boles demonic faces screwed up in hate and fury. *This is still the land of the old Droys, begone from it while you are still unharmed!*

Roy Bean whistled tunelessly through his buck teeth, a

habit of his when he experienced a sense of inferiority. He almost always whistled on shooting days when he was surrounded by the visiting gentry with their Range Rovers and Purdey or Boss guns. Deep down he hated them, hated his own role which was to serve. Sometimes when this obsession really got the better of him he would take his .22 rifle, fitted with a silencer, up to the feeding points in the woods and pick off a few handsome cock pheasants as they pecked the grain he had thrown down for them. Rader, the butcher in town, would always give him a few quid for birds on the side. It could cost the gamekeeper his job if he was found out, but he told himself that the risk was outweighed by the satisfaction of nicking half a dozen brace of the Agent's birds. It got him one up on the bastards and made him smarter than them.

Old Houliston had had a fright, the keeper could tell from just looking at him, the way his ruddiness had paled, his hands shaking slightly as he fidgeted with his stick. Those two had seen something in there they didn't like. But no way was Roy Bean going to go back to the old house to find out. No, sir!

He wished he could have carried his gun today. Damn it, he had every right to because Droy Wood was officially part of his game preserves. But that officious Superintendent had made him leave it behind in the van. "Any guns, gamekeeper, will be carried by police marksmen only." Yes, sir. Fuck you.

The going was harder now, the reed-beds denser, the ground softer. Roy Bean used his long ash stick to prod the area in front of him, trying to find the firmer patches. This fog was getting thicker, too; you couldn't see the man on your right or left any longer, and the line could not close up any more or they would not be able to cover the terrain systematically.

At least that Superintendent had not objected to him bringing Muffin, the springer spaniel, along. Roy didn't feel right going anywhere without a dog on the estate. A day in rough cover like this would do her good, cool her ardor. She never walked, always ran; never stopped searching for a scent. If any of the missing people were in here Muffin would find them, long before those snarling police dogs did. Nevertheless, with the fog coming down like this he would have felt a lot easier with a gun under his arm. Christ, he only hoped that they had drawn it all before dark.

The liver and white springer had gone on ahead, probably on a rabbit scent. Roy whistled urgently. Hell, he didn't want her getting lost in *here*. No response, but he could hear her thrashing and splashing about in the rushes up ahead. He whistled again.

Suddenly the spaniel bitch stopped, a second or two of silence and then she gave a cry, a yelp . . . Whimpering, yelping again.

"Muffin!" Roy Bean stepped forward, felt himself sink into a patch of quagmire, the mud viciously sucking at him as though it sought to pull him down below the surface. "Fucking hell!"

Fear, anger, and even as he floundered, caught hold of a silver birch seedling, he saw the spaniel coming back. Her ears were flat on her head, her tail curled between her legs, running, whining and whimpering. Fleeing!

"You stupid fucking bitch!" If his feet had not been so firmly embedded in the mud, Roy Bean would have kicked out at her. She ran up to him, came up close behind him. "Stupid bugger, you'll knock me back in there. You'll . . ."

His anger trailed off as he glimpsed a movement in the fog ahead of him, a shape materializing out of the swirling gray vapor. A man. At first he thought it was one of the search party, a soldier or policeman, perhaps, who had heard his struggles in the bog and come to investigate.

But no, the silhouette was wrong, the strange ill-fitting coat, the triangular-shaped hat with long matted hair falling from beneath it like a cartoonist's impression of a living scarecrow. And for a second, maybe two, Roy Bean was afforded a glimpse of the face and he almost screamed. Coarse features, partially bearded as though mange had taken its toll, sunken sockets that were eyeless yet saw; the mouth open in a snarl of anger displaying a double row of broken blackened teeth.

And then it was gone, as suddenly as it had come, fading back into the fog as though it had never been. A trick of the half-light, the fog? Roy Bean would have settled for that explanation, told himself over and over again that it was an illusion, had it not been for the spaniel cringing and whimpering up against him.

He knew only too well that whatever that thing was it existed.

Dusk was beginning to merge with the thickening fog as the searchers finally emerged from the village end of Droy Wood, weary, mud-splattered soldiers and policemen, physically and mentally exhausted, the tracker dogs staying close to their masters. Nobody spoke, merely glanced dejectedly at one another, clustering together, waiting for the Superintendent to come across and dismiss them.

Three missing people: a conservation officer, an attractive naked girl and a crazed sex killer were not in Droy Wood.

But everybody sensed that *something* was.

FOUR

Curled up against the bole of that dead tree Carol Embleton slept fitfully. And dreamed. An erotic, frightening dream.

She was in a room, a dark gloomy place with no windows, sprawled on the cold stone floor. Naked. A man stood over her, legs astride, and glancing up she saw that he was naked, too. And aroused.

Despair, then hope as she made out his features. Andy! Oh thank God! Until she saw his expression, the flushed angry cheeks, the blazing eyes, the lips curled in a contemptuous sneer.

"You bitch!" He kicked her with his bare foot, brought a gasp of pain from her lips, had her cringing, throwing up an arm to protect her head in anticipation of another blow. "You dirty little poxy whore!"

Why, Andy, please tell me *why?*

"You're going to bloody well answer my question and I want the truth!" Furious, squatting on his haunches, a fist bunched threateningly.

"I'll tell you," she sobbed. "I'll tell you anything you want to know. I will!"

"You'd better." His face was thrust closer to hers and she smelled his breath. He had been eating peppermints again. "You've been masturbating, haven't you? *Answer me!*"

"Yes." Shame welled up inside, the tears came in a flood. "I have. And I'm sorry."

"Cow!" His fist caught her across the mouth, jerked her head back. "And you weren't a virgin when I fucked you the first time. *Were you*?"

"No." Shuddering, almost on the verge of hysteria. "I wasn't a virgin. You know that, I told you."

"Then tell me again."

"It was a lad out of the village." She pressed herself back against the cold wet wall, rough stonework gouging her shoulder blades. "Just the once. I swear it was only the once."

"And then you were soliciting on the roadside at night, getting picked up by motorists, getting screwed on the backseat. Weren't you? For Christ's sake, weren't you?"

"No!"

"Fucking liar!" Andy Dark's fist smashed aside Carol's frail defenses, took her on the side of the jaw. She felt her teeth rattle, tasted blood. Oh Andy, I love you, you don't have to . . . "What about that guy in the Mini after the disco. You rode him like you hadn't had any cock for a month. *Didn't you*?"

"No . . . yes . . . Oh God, I had to, I swear I had to. He'd have killed me otherwise. He raped me."

Suddenly the room was much darker so that she could not see Andy anymore, only feel him. Strong hands gripping her, hurting her, splaying her back on the floor, banging her head on the stones as he came on top of her. Thrusting her, slapping, cursing, and breathing peppermint all over her. "And when I've finished fucking you I'm going to kill you. You won't get away this time!"

Her brain spun, she felt herself going into a faint, starting to slide over the brink of that bottomless black abyss. Every bone in her body ached but she didn't mind the physical hurt. If only Andy . . .

Andy . . . Andy . . . An . . . dy . . .

She awoke crying, shivering with cold, staring into the blackness of a rain-soaked autumn night, still calling for Andy Dark until realization filtered through her bemused brain. He wasn't here, he wasn't going to come. But he wouldn't do anything like that to her. Furthermore, he never ate peppermints.

Everything came back to her. She was naked and alone in Droy Wood and there was a sex killer somewhere around. Furthermore, she was lost and she would have to stay here until daylight. The tears out of her dream were still wet on her face and now she let them come with full spate.

Gradually she became aware of a noise. At first she thought it was thunder, a resonant rumbling that vibrated the air, the distant sky lit up by vivid flashes that merged into a bright fiery glow. Almost dazzling if you looked at it long enough; frightening because you didn't know what it was.

It was heavy gunfire, she came to that conclusion. And those shuddering explosions were bombs going off with incessant devastating force. The whole city was ablaze; she could even smell the acrid smoke in the air. Heavy aircraft droned, wave after wave of them . . . Oh God, another war had broken out. This night, the whole world had gone crazy. Unless it was only another nightmare like the last one.

That droning noise was louder, much louder. Carol Embleton cowered, instinctively hugged the lichen-covered tree trunk against which she rested. One of the planes was coming this way, flying as low as those small pilotless aircraft sometimes did during training sessions across the coastline. Louder, deafening.

She saw it the moment it burst into flames, a blinding flash, blazing debris, a sharp nosedive; clapped her hands over her ears in anticipation of the devastating explosion. The sky was a deep scarlet hue, surely a reflection of hellfire itself.

She trembled, cowered. This was madness and she was mad, too. Staring skyward with frightened eyes, smelling the burning and in her mind hearing the screams of the tormented. Scudding fiery clouds deluging rain as though they were determined to douse the inferno. Something attracted her attention; at first she thought it was a weird shadow cast by the distant flickering flames. The moon showed itself briefly and in that instant she recognized the drifting silhouette, the billowing silk, the taut ropes which supported the man. A parachutist!

Amazement, relief that he had escaped from that plane crash, searching the smoky sky for others but seeing none, experiencing again her own fear of flying. Air disasters filled her with a sense of horror; in a road accident you stood a chance but up there you had none, plummeted earthward to certain death.

The parachutist became invisible against the low cloud, possibly he had already landed, maybe he was caught up in the treetops, entangled in his trappings, hanging suspended from the branches, helpless. Or else he was lying hurt, a broken limb, unconscious, drowning in one of these shallow pools of water.

One thought after another tumbled into her bemused brain. And amid them a spark of hope glowed. An ally, somebody who would help her in return for being helped. An *ally!* Together they would find a way out of this dreadful place, he would protect her from the rapist. She must try and find the lone survivor from that plane at once, brave the bogs and the darkness.

And the fog!

She had not noticed the mist creeping in. It had crept

stealthily, silently across the wood under cover of darkness and she only became aware of it now that the moon was showing itself intermittently. Gray tentacles of vapor curling around the tree boles, touching her with their cold clammy outstretched fingers as though to ensnare her. *This is the land of the damned and you shall not escape.*

Carol Embleton broke into a run, heedless of the squelching mud. The trees around her became moving living things, slapping at her with low branches, reeds clutching at her bare ankles as though to drag her down into their evil mire. *Come, join us for eternity in our stinking cold mud.*

She blundered into a deep bog, somehow extricated herself, found a way round it. Running breathlessly, blindly, not knowing if she headed in the right direction, only that she had to keep going. A lurking fear that her attacker might suddenly spring out on her for surely he must have heard her by now. She had to find that strange parachutist, only then would she be safe.

Suddenly her flight was brought to an abrupt halt. She would have screamed her sheer terror aloud had not a cold wet hand been clapped over her mouth and nostrils with asphyxiating force. Another arm encircled her body, lifted her up off the ground.

And in that moment she gave in, surrendered to whatever Fate had ordained. The fox had given the hounds a good run for their money and now, exhausted, accepted the inevitable. She was going to die, she prayed that it would be quick, that whatever he was going to do to her he would inflict upon her corpse, spare her the terror and the shame of undergoing a second rape.

"Mein Gott!"

She heard the thick nasal tones as she was flung to the

ground, sodden marsh grass breaking her fall, lying there with her eyes tightly shut, not wanting to look up into that crazed lusting expression again.

"Kill me," she whimpered. "Don't play with me. Do what you want after I am dead."

Silence. She was aware of the mist fingers exploring her obscenely, trying to prise her thighs apart, evil aiding evil. She felt the penetrating stare of her attacker, heard his breathing.

"Mein Gott!" Again, unfamiliar, a ring of amazement in the voice. In a strange sort of way it was reassuring.

Fearfully Carol Embleton opened her eyes, gazed uncomprehendingly at the man who stood looking down upon her, the mist hanging back from him as though in some way it was afraid to approach him.

Close-cropped blond hair, his figure made bulky by the thick flying suit he wore, the padded jacket ripped, the material hanging down in ribbons. High cheekbones, a nasty gash just below the left one but it appeared to have stopped bleeding. Heavy knee-length boots dripping foul marsh mud. The patchy moonlight glinted on something metal in his hand and with a start she identified the object, a pistol, the barrel trained unwaveringly on herself.

For several seconds the two of them stared at each other and finally it was the stranger who spoke, slowly as though he had to search some long-forgotten vocabulary to produce words in the English language.

"What is it that you do here?"

"I . . . I . . ."

"Answer me. Quickly." The pistol jerked threateningly.

"I'm lost." Carol swallowed. She had to be mad, this awful wood had snapped her mind playing cruel tricks on her. And then she remembered the parachutist who had come drifting down out of the sky. If that had really happened then this must be him.

"A whore plying her trade in a marsh wood by night." He laughed humorlessly. "A trick to lure me by the mad British who persist in fighting a hopeless war."

"I . . . don't understand." Oh God, he was a madman too. "I was attacked. Raped. I fled in here, got lost. I saw your plane crash. I thought that together we could escape . . ."

"It *is* a trick," he said, advancing a step, and for one awful moment she thought that the finger on that trigger was going to tighten, blast her into instant oblivion. "The British have tried many tricks to capture me. Sometimes they send men in sailing boats from the sea, a ridiculous ploy. Other times they dress as ancient worshippers, but still Bertie Hass remains at large, for a Nazi is no fool."

"A Nazi!"

"You still persist with this ridiculous story." There was a note of anger in his tone now. "But an honored member of the Führer's Luftwaffe is above the temptation of a common whore. Your trick has failed and now you must pay for your folly. On your feet!"

Shakily Carol struggled to her feet. She had to be mad but she had no choice other than to obey this mysterious gunman. She stumbled, felt something hard boring into her back. The fog was so thick now that she could not see more than a yard or two in front of her yet her companion seemed oblivious to it, an urgency about him as though he knew exactly where he was going. But that was impossible, he had only landed a short while ago!

It had stopped raining now and the moonlight was fighting to infiltrate the thick mist. And far away she could still hear those continuous explosions.

Suddenly she saw the building looming up before her, a

huge castlelike edifice with high turrets, sinister in the gloom. The only house in Droy Wood is Droy House, she thought, and they reckon it's no more than a shell these days, but this was sound with no signs of decay.

"My castle," he said with pride in his voice as he pulled up sharply, grasping her wrist in an icy grip as though he feared lest she might decide to make a dash for freedom. "Just as the Führer has his Crow's Nest so Bertie Hass has his own impregnable refuge. The British have not found it for here it is screened from them, protected by the wood and the marshes."

"But . . . but the war's been over for almost forty years!" She turned to face him. "In 1945. This is 1980 . . ."

"Fool!" For one moment she thought he was going to strike her across the face. "The war is *nearly* over, the stubborn British and their allies still believing that they can thwart the advance of the Master Race. I have served the Fatherland and it is my lot to remain here in this place until the might of Germany finally overthrows Britain."

She nodded dumbly; to argue further would have been to invite swift retribution.

"Now let us go inside." The Luger prodded her forward again. "You will remain here as my prisoner." He laughed, a hollow sound that had her naked flesh goosepimpling. "Indeed, I, too, am a prisoner here until the German army comes to release me."

There was no visible sign of ruin inside the building, just bare stone walls and floors, empty of furniture, cold and eerie. Moonlight shafted in through a window, illuminating the hall, and something fluttered in the shadows —squeaked as though protesting at this intrusion. Bats, Carol grimaced. There were probably rats, too.

A flight of steps going downward. She would have fallen had not the man who called himself Bertie Hass caught her. His fingers were deathly cold like the touch of dead flesh: a corpse. An overpowering stench of dank staleness had her coughing, an almost airless atmosphere down here that was icy cold. She felt cobwebs brush her, adhere to her face and hair, the rough floor scraping the soles of her feet as her captor dragged her with him. Impenetrable blackness all around her.

She felt something cold and hard encircle her wrist, snap and tighten with a metallic click, could not hold back her whimper of fear. Her other arm was seized, pinioned to the wall behind her in the same way. Instinctively she struggled but no way could she prevent her ankles being manacled. Straining, hearing chains rattle, only too well aware that she was fastened to the wall.

"Please . . ." she sobbed.

"If you scream nobody will hear you." The German's voice was a whisper in the darkness. "Here you will remain, a prisoner of war . . . A *spy*." Venom, hatred. "Perhaps when the German army arrives you will be executed as such. I cannot say, for such a decision will be left to the Gestapo. You will not have long to wait. The cities of your country are being razed to the ground by the devastating raids of the Luftwaffe, Britain totters on the brink of defeat."

Fanaticism. She thought she caught a click of heels, visualized an upraised hand, a Nazi salute. Then he was leaving her, a fast walk. Marching. Self-discipline even in madness.

Oh please God this is all some terrible nightmare. She strained at her manacles but they were real enough. She was just able to stand, the balls of her feet touching the dungeon floor, her arms already beginning to go numb as the blood drained from them.

Andy, where are you? I'm sorry; if I hadn't lost my temper with you this would never have happened. But Andy Dark wasn't likely to find her here; nobody was.

Something brushed against her feet and she let out a scream as she felt the rough fur of a moving body, heard scuffling sounds. Her eyesight had adjusted to the darkness and now she saw a myriad of dull red pinpoints like minute unpolished rubies set out on a black cloth. Rats! Dozens of them, just squatting in the corners watching her; waiting until she was carrion to feed on. She wondered if they might attack her while she still lived, tear at her flesh with their tiny sharp teeth. But at the moment they seemed prepared to be patient.

There was a roaring in Carol's ears, the echoes of the bombing raid lingering, the staccato return fire from the sparse defenses. A red haze before her eyes, the reflections in a night sky of a burning city. The constant drone of heavy aircraft; the smell of burning in her nostrils.

Exhaustion again, her body sagging so that her wrists hurt as they took the strain. And her recent nightmare came back to her, this same stone-walled cell of hopelessness. An interrogator who might have been Andy. Or James Foster.

Or Bertie Hass.

"You dirty whore, answer my questions!"

"No, *please!*"

Jerking back into awful wakefulness, seeing that the rats had moved in closer.

FIVE

Still that trail of broken, trodden-down reeds wove on ahead of Andy Dark. In places it backtracked where the mud was too deep and only his keen eyesight picked up the trail again. Every time he came upon a patch of dense undergrowth he paused to part the foliage, steeled himself to search it, afraid of what he might see. But there was nothing.

Surely they had not come *this* far? In places he found the heavier tracks where the man had followed in blind crazed pursuit but in the pitch darkness of night Foster had been unable to see the tracks which would have led him to the girl.

Through a long narrow stretch of thick reeds and out again on to wet but firm ground; veering to the right, back again to the left, and then he came upon that patch of ground beneath the aged and rotting tree where Carol had spent the night, saw how the springy grass had been flattened, had barely started to straighten up again. A matter of only an hour or two ago perhaps.

His pulses were racing, there was a roaring in his ears. She had still been alive then, the killer had not found her. Perhaps with the coming of daylight she had made her way back toward the road. She might be home already, his own mission a fool's errand.

And then he saw the tracks again leading off in the opposite direction; eastward, seaward. Oh Christ Almighty, she had lost all sense of direction, had blundered off toward the marshes. She . . .

He stopped, a movement catching his eye amid the darkness of the trees. A wisp like smoke, as though somebody unseen had lit a cigarette. Not dispersing, thickening; more of it, billowing.

The fog was coming in from the sea again!

He leaned his body up against a tree, wrestled with his decision. It needed an army to search Droy Wood effectively. Carol was lost already, maybe panicking. She would wander around in circles forever, deep bogs cutting off what seemed to be the obvious exits. And with the mist coming down anything could happen. The rapist was in here, too. Oh Jesus!

Andy Dark cupped his hands, yelled, "Carol . . . *Carol.*"

Nothing, not even an echo. Just the mist thickening with unbelievable rapidity. He sighed, remembered all those stories about the wood. Every place had its legends, stories spread and added to by superstitious locals. The villagers were scared of Droy Wood but there were logical reasons for keeping away. Deep bogs that could suck you down if you panicked and floundered in them, these damnable mists, caused by the adjacent gaseous marshes, doubled the perils. The dangers were only too *real.*

"Ca-rol!"

He was wasting his breath. Just a cloying silence everywhere, the old trees dripping with condensation. He ought to go for help but that would take time, maybe an hour before he got back to the village, God knows how long to muster a search party, and it could be late afternoon by the time they got back here. Then darkness, another night in this awful place for Carol. No, it wasn't on, he must carry on searching, pray that he found her.

He looked at his watch. 9:25. No, that couldn't possibly be right, he had been in here much longer than that. Holding it to his ear, shaking it, tapping it. Sod it, his watch had stopped and with this damned mist drifting in like this it was difficult to even guess what time of day it was.

Andy set off, wished that he had a compass with him, the one he always used when he went bird watching on the marshes. But he didn't and he would have to make the best of it. The tracks were becoming erratic now as though Carol had had several changes of mind, met up with a wide channel and tried to find a shallow crossing, eventually finding somewhere to cross.

It took him several minutes to find where she had crossed over; a sluggish black stream that came up to the tops of his Wellington boots, slopped over once and wet his socks. The mud was sticky, pulling back on every step he took until finally he reached the opposite bank. He clambered out, looking for a continuation of the trail he was following. It wasn't there, *not a single imprint of Carol Embleton's feet in the squelchy black silt.*

There had to be! He looked about him, his task being made doubly difficult by the encroaching mist. He walked ten yards to his right, found nothing and retraced his steps. Tried the left; nothing again.

Perplexed, worried. There *had* to be tracks unless she had followed the course of this stream. Upstream or down? He sighed, then tensed as a faint noise caught his ears, some kind of movement, a long-dead branch snapping, a squelching footstep.

Andy Dark tried to see through the fog but it was thicker than ever now, visibility reduced to a maximum of ten yards or so. He heard the noise again, almost like long wheezing breaths, somebody who moved with difficulty. Certainly not Carol; in that case it had to be . . . the rapist!

Anger, hatred welled up inside Andy. Only yards away from him was the man who had subjected Carol Embleton to terrors beyond male comprehension. She might even be . . . dead! The conservancy officer experienced a wave of dizziness at the thought. He might be too late, the mutilated body already sucked down by a vile bog. Gone forever.

The bastard! Andy moved forward, fists clenched. He would make the fucker pay for what he'd done, mete out a punishment beyond the laws of civilization. The other would scream for mercy, but there would be none. No softly administered legislature, no protection from the fury of an outraged public. Here in Droy Wood it would be man against man, the death penalty the sentence imposed upon a sex killer; Andy Dark judge, jury and executioner.

His face was twisted into a mask of malevolence, moving cautiously in the direction from where the sounds had come, through stunted spreading oaks whose boughs no longer sprouted foliage, a dead silent world of murk and rancid marsh odors.

Andy tensed, caught sight of a fleeting shape in the mist, grunted with bewilderment. He had expected to see a naked man whose clothes remained in the parked roadside Mini after he had satisfied his lust. Instead he saw a long coat, a three-cornered shaped hat, the fashion of a bygone age. A silhouette that merged with the gray swirling vapor and was lost again. He hurried forward, paused once more to listen. Squelching footsteps going away from him, hurrying, seeming to traverse patches of bog that Andy had to circumnavigate. *And leaving no tracks in his wake . . .*

Andy Dark sweated profusely but somehow he could not catch the other up. Just fleeting glimpses as the man in front forged ahead into the fog, never once glancing back, no suspicion of pursuit. The sweat on Andy's body chilled; there was something uncannily inexplicable about this, *the way the other crossed deep bogs and left not a single broken reed to mark his passage!*

And suddenly Andy was aware of other movements around him, the tramping of feet, the splashing of water. Voices, muffled shouts but he did not understand the tongue, more like animal grunts. Frightening, recalling again the old legends, of happenings in here when the mists came in off the marshes and people disappeared never to be seen again. Rubbish! Somehow he could not convince himself of that right now, was prepared to believe things which he would have scoffed at in the safety of his own office back at the bungalow.

He stopped, pressed himself flat against the nearest tree. Two men, only yards apart, emerged from the trees close by, passed within feet of him. Oh Jesus wept, you only had to see those faces, even partially obscured by the mist, to know that something was dreadfully wrong. Gaunt and wizened, the features of long-dead corpses, decomposition just beginning to set in, dressed in long greatcoats, those triangular hats pulled well down as though they wished to spare any hidden watcher the horror of looking upon their putrid countenances.

Passing him and going on, heading in the same direction as the first one. *And there were more of them, Andy could hear them to the right and left of him. Fear of a different kind now, not just for Carol Embleton's safety, but the terror of being alone in this dreadful wood with things that had no place in the realms of the living world!*

He smelled the marshes and the sea shortly before the

weird trees petered out, the fog not so dark now. They were out in the open, heading directly toward the sea. Andy paused, doubted the wisdom of following, yet Carol might be out there. He prayed to God that she wasn't but he could not chance it.

Moving cautiously, stooping low even though the fog hid him, following the progress of the others by ear. Some urgent calling had brought them out on to Droy marshes, some terrible purpose to be fulfilled which he was about to witness.

Suddenly he almost blundered into them, checked just in time, ducked back into the fog. There were half a dozen of them crouched behind boulders on the narrow rocky shore, their backs to him, their attention focused seaward, otherwise they would almost certainly have seen him. Lurking, waiting. For what?

Andy Dark dropped onto his haunches. The fog seemed to thicken as though to screen something from him which he had no right to witness, blanking out even those creatures purporting to be men in a land of mist. They were no longer communicating with each other in those guttural grunts, kneeling silently amid the stinking heaps of seaweed. Watching.

Then his ears picked up a sound, the soft rhythmic splashing of water, one which he instantly recognized as that of oars being pulled, heading inshore.

Beyond Andy Dark's vision a rowing boat was steadily coming inshore from the open sea.

SIX

"Your part in the reconstruction of events leading up to the disappearance of Miss Embleton and Mr. Dark must be entirely voluntary, Miss Brown. I want you to understand that." Detective-Sergeant Jim Fillery regarded the girl seated in his temporary headquarters at Droy police station. He didn't want any repercussions, any flak from the media if anything went wrong. Not that it was likely to but he could just as easily have got a plainclothes WPC to take the role. This girl would be better, though, the locals would take a greater interest, it might jog a memory somewhere along the fast-cooling trail which had begun at the disco. In all probability it wouldn't throw anything up but at least you were seen to be doing something. And, frankly, at the moment Jim Fillery could not think of anything else. Three people who should have been found in Droy Wood, and the search had been a very thorough one, had literally vanished into thin air.

"I want to do it." Thelma Brown smiled. "Carol was my best friend and after all I was one of the last people to see her."

"Fair enough." Fillery nodded. "You'll be under supervision the whole time so you don't need to worry. We'll start tonight, the same disco, the same sequence of records, and hopefully everybody who was there last time will come again. Then you'll leave at 11:30, walk the same route, and one of our officers will pick you up in a blue Mini and drive you to the edge of Droy Wood. That'll be the end of the reconstruction." Christ, we can't have you running off into the wood.

All the same, Thelma Brown was nervous. Suddenly she was playing a leading role in the recent events which had shocked the whole of Droy village. Yet she felt a duty toward Carol, the need to do something positive.

"You're mad," her mother had retorted angrily when she heard of the proposed reconstruction. "No good can come of this. And it's making your father ill." Emotional blackmail; Thelma had been subjected to it all her life. "Now don't you get stopping out late at nights because your father can't go to sleep until you're safely in, and getting overtired at his age isn't good for him."

John, her boyfriend, was furious too. "I won't let you do it!" He confronted her angrily, his flushed cheeks matching his red hair, fists clenched. "You're not bloody well going, d'you hear?"

"I'll do as I please," Thelma Brown retorted, "and neither you nor anybody else will stop me."

"It's crazy, it's dangerous and it won't do any good." He was beginning to raise his voice now. "These reconstructions never work out, they're just a waste of everybody's time. Like these identikit pictures the police are always issuing, an artist's impression of the killer taken from scraps of information they get from unreliable witnesses, and when they finally catch the guy he looks nothing like his picture. They set all these things up to convince the public they're doing something because otherwise they wouldn't have a bloody clue."

"I'm going," she said stubbornly, "whether you like it or not and if you don't, you know what you can do!"

So the following night Thelma Brown walked nervously into that crowded disco in the village hall, a loner who was going to jive on her own all night.

Rocking all over the world.

Trying to pick up the mood. My name is Carol Embleton. *Carol Embleton.* John's over there, can't take his eyes off you. John? Oh yes, Thelma Brown's boyfriend. Can't see Thelma but there's so many people here it's difficult to be sure; could be they've had another tiff and he's come on his own. It's none of my business anyway because I'm engaged to Andy Dark. A little ripple started to goosepimple her skin. It was an exciting fantasy.

Another record, an even faster beat, the lights dimmed so that those flashing colored bulbs dazzled you, transported you into a world of cavorting shadows and ear-bursting music. Like it had been the other night; exactly the same.

You've got to go at 11:30 because you're walking home tonight. On your own. Where's Andy? Gone filming something or other. You're walking the long way round tonight, along by Droy Wood . . . Her pulses were hammering faster than that double bass now. She hadn't thought it would be quite so *real* as this. Sounded fine in the cold sober light of an October morning; but now it was dark outside, probably raining too. She shivered. It wasn't such a good idea after all.

The clothes she was wearing, they were all Carol's, the ones they had found in that Mini: jeans, blouse-top, the sheepskin hanging up in the ladies . . . the clothes that had been torn from Carol's body before . . . Oh God!

No, they can't be because *you're* Carol and nothing has happened to you and it isn't likely to. Just a long walk home in the dark, you'll have done your bit then. Turning so that her back was to that psychedelic lighting, having to wait for her eyes to stop flashing blue, green and yellow before she could make out the hands of the clock on the wall. 11:25. Thelma Brown's stomach seemed to flip then consolidated into a hard ball, brought with it a fleeting sensation of dizziness. This is it, you're on your way, girl!

The calves of her legs felt spongy as she pushed her way through the jiving mass of bodies, heading toward the door marked "ladies." A sickening smell of strong mixed perfumes and urine as she scraped the door back, shut it again. That sheepskin coat, the real McCoy, one that Andy Dark had bought her for . . . for an engagement present. Just a shade too big across the shoulders but that didn't matter.

Some graffiti on the wall, an almost illegible scribble in pencil by some dirty slut, probably one of those motorbike guys' girls—"do *you* masturbate?" Thelma found herself blushing, swallowing, a direct question that seemed to leap off the peeling emulsion at her. Mind your own bloody business.

She felt a forest of eyes on her as she made her way toward the exit. Everybody's watching you. So what? They're probably wondering why Andy isn't here, wondering if they can make some gossip out of it.

Outside the sky was beginning to cloud over, the moon fast becoming buried but fighting hard to shine through the gathering formation. For a second or two it was clear and if you looked at it hard enough there was a face up there just like they used to tell you when you were a kid. Frowning. You shouldn't be walking home on your own tonight, Thelma Brown *(sorry, Carol Embleton)*. But if you must, don't go by Droy Wood. Strange things happen to people who get caught up when the mists roll across.

I must.

The wind was getting up, scattering early fallen leaves,

blowing them along the road as though some invisible giant were sweeping them with a broom. There was a hint of drizzle in the atmosphere and Thelma turned up her collar, began to walk quickly. It shouldn't take all that long, and anyway the Mini will pick you up soon. You're not supposed to know about the Mini.

A row of cottages on either side of the road, again that feeling of being watched although most of them were in darkness. Faces pressed against window panes, fogging up the glass. See, there she goes. That's Carol Embleton on her last walk. She won't be seen again. Ever.

A sudden squall of cold autumn rain had Thelma wanting to break into a run. Don't go by Droy Wood. It's not too late, you can chuck it in now, tell that CID man that it was too much for you. They can't *make* you do it.

I will do it, I'm not turning back, and I'm going along by Droy Wood, as far as the stile in the hedge and then I'll cut back across the fields. Half an hour and I'll be home.

The village was behind her now, just wet tarmac glinting in the struggling moonlight and hedges that bent over in the wind, tall wispy hawthorn that had not been trimmed for two or three seasons. Driving rain smacked the back of her legs as though whipping her forward. Hurry, it's too late to turn back now. You'll have to pass Droy Wood.

And then she heard the car coming. Walk in the road in case he doesn't see you and passes you by. If that happens you'll have to pass the wood on your own.

The driver was taking his time, idling like he was curb-crawling. His lights hadn't reached her yet. She experienced uneasiness bordering on fear. This was how it had been for Carol (me), just not knowing for sure who was driving that car. Suppose it wasn't the policeman; he hadn't left the village yet. Somebody else. Jump in, darling, it's nice and dry in here.

Then the beams of the headlights hit her, overtook her, bounced back at her with dazzling brightness off the wall of low-lying mist which had rolled in across the road ahead of her. The car was going faster now, catching her up. Braking, a squeal of rubber on wet tarmac, the Mini level with her, the passenger door swinging open.

"Jump in, darling, out of the wet."

She hesitated, the urge strong to run. No, I'm not getting in because that's what happened to Carol. Holding on to the door, trying to make out the shadowy figure inside. Just a silhouette, a cardboard outline, it could have been anybody.

"C'mon, you're getting soaked." She detected a slight impatience in the other's voice. Don't keep me waiting because . . . It was the "because" that worried her. Nevertheless she slid into the seat, pulled the door shut.

"And what brings you out on a night like this, darling?" She thought she detected a faint whiff of peppermint. Chewing gum probably because policemen weren't allowed to smoke on duty.

"I . . . I'm walking home." Well, that was bloody obvious enough. "My boyfriend didn't go to the disco tonight so I went on my own. I didn't enjoy it, though." True.

"Damn this fog." Her companion swung the car hard over to the left, dipped his lights and focused the nearside beam on the verge. "You have to be prepared for low-lying pockets of fog this time of the year, particularly alongside marshy places. I expect we'll run out of it in a minute or two."

"Probably." Once we're clear of Droy Wood.

"What's your name?" She sensed him glancing quickly

at her. He knew, he had to; but it was an act, all the way through.

"Thel . . . Carol Embleton." In for a penny, in for a pound, act the whole thing through. This was getting eerie though, the fog thickening now, swirling around the slow-moving car as if it were trying to get to the occupants.

"You live round here?"

"Yes." You know bloody well I do. "You can drop me off a bit farther up the road . . . past the wood. There's a stile in the hedge there. It'll only take me a few minutes to get home from there."

But, of course, he wouldn't be dropping her off by the stile. They would be turning into that rutted lay-by alongside the wood. What then, did they turn round and go home? Surely they would, there wouldn't be much gained by sitting out there half the night, Thelma thought.

Silence as he attempted to negotiate the dense fog, down to 15 mph now. She stole a glance at him, saw his features reflected in the light from the facia. No more than thirty, handsome in a rugged kind of way. Tough. She couldn't make out exactly what he was wearing but in all probability they were the clothes belonging to that man James Foster. Revulsion at the thought, how could he? Because he was a policeman and got paid for doing unpleasant things that other people didn't like doing. Thelma found herself edging away from him, pressing herself against the door. This was what it had been like for Carol, in the car with a sex killer. But this man's a policeman. Are you sure? How do you *know* he's a policeman? He *has* to be. No, he doesn't.

And then he was swinging the car across the road, driving through a wafting sea of fog, all landmarks obscured, the vapor swirling across the windscreen. Thelma clutched at her seat, almost screamed. "God, you can't possibly see where you're going. We'll go off the road, crash, overturn."

But they didn't. The Mini bumped across ruts, slewed in thick mud, and came to a standstill on the lay-by adjacent to Droy Wood. A few seconds' pause and then the headlights were switched off, the engine seeming to take an age to die, leaving just the faint eerie glow from the sidelights and the facia illuminations.

You could almost feel the fog seeping in through ill-fitting doors, touching you obscenely, mocking you. Threatening you. Thelma's relief was short-lived. They hadn't crashed, somehow the driver had found the place they were looking for. And now it was all over, she could go home.

"This is the place." It was a statement not a question from the policeman.

"Yes." Her voice sounded unfamiliar, far away. She was trembling, felt sick. "That's it . . . isn't it?"

"We don't know." His voice was flat, expressionless. "It all depends on the fog."

"What . . . whatever do you mean?" Icy fingers clutched at Thelma Brown's heart, almost stopped it then speeded it back up to full speed; thumping, pulse pounding.

"The fog," his tone didn't alter, "we can't very well go anywhere, can we?"

His words spun in her brain, a record with a chipped groove, the stylus sticking. *We can't very well go anywhere . . . We can't . . .*

"We . . . you could reverse out on to the road . . . find the verge . . . follow it. Couldn't you?"

"This fog's getting thicker." That was certainly true,

you couldn't even see the reflection of the sidelights now. "It would be stupid, dangerous. We'll just have to sit it out."

Something about his tone frightened her, a kind of gloating, the elements doing just what he wanted them to. I'm sorry, Auntie Winnie, we can't come to tea today because of the weather. Thank God; a ready-made excuse.

"We can't stop here." Thelma's voice was a whisper of hopelessness.

"Why not? It's not exactly cold, just damp and foggy, and if we do get cold I can always run the engine."

Suddenly Thelma stiffened, felt an arm coming round her, strong fingers gripping her shoulders, pulling her gently but firmly toward the driver's seat; lips came in search of her own, found them in a kiss to which she did not respond, tasted peppermint again.

"Please . . ." She tried to move away but he was holding her too tightly.

"You're a very attractive girl." Smooth, frightening tones. "And we can stop here all night. Just you and me, and nobody will ask any questions. They can't come looking for us in this, can they?"

Thelma's mouth was dry. He was holding her chin now, making sure she could not turn her head away from him, forcing her to look into his eyes. Eyes that glowed with a strange green hue. It was the reflection from the dashboard lights, it had to be. Even so he didn't look like she had at first thought. Rugged certainly, but something else—ruthless, vicious. She shivered, was reminded how Carol must have felt. But I'm not Carol, I'm Thelma Brown, and this isn't real. It's a mock-up, an act. This man's a policeman, he'll look after me. But the expression in his eyes said different.

"My boyfriend will come looking for me," she said. "He didn't like me coming in the first place."

"You've got a boyfriend!" He seemed surprised, excited.

"Yes." What else was there to say?

"I'll bet you're not a virgin then." Thelma sensed rather than saw the leer. Fear and embarrassment blended and those words on the wall of that dingy ladies' room back at the village hall flashed before her eyes. Blushing, shuddering, knowing that she had to answer him.

"No, I'm not a virgin." His lips were coming after her again, the smell of peppermint almost overpowering. She tried to struggle but his grip tightened, brought a cry of pain from her. "Stop it, you're hurting me."

But he didn't stop, pressing her back in the seat, crushing his mouth against hers, his tongue pushing at her until she opened up to let him push it into her in a simulation of the sex act. Rape!

Thelma was on the verge of tears now, gasping for breath when he withdrew, seeing those lusting eyes boring into her own, seeming to read her thoughts. She wanted to scream, to yell, "How dare you, I'm going to report you to Sergeant Fillery" but she didn't. For the same reasons that Carol Embleton hadn't screamed in the car a few nights ago.

"I don't want you to," she sobbed.

"But *I* want to." His voice was a deep whisper, a very purposeful frightening one. Somehow her sheepskin coat had come unbuttoned and now the fingers of his free hand were smoothing over her blouse, dwelling on the soft curves of her breasts. "We've got a whole night ahead of us, darling."

Too scared to resist, moving her body so that he could

slide her clothes off, trembling as he fondled her. Watching as he undressed himself, knowing that there was no way she could make a dash for freedom, aware of that awful fog drifting across the windows like some perverted voyeur.

He lifted her into a kneeling position, head and shoulders drooped over the back of the passenger seat, staring down at the well of the rear seat, a black abyss that seemed to beckon her. Crying, her body screaming protests as this stranger took her from behind, satisfied his lust.

Slowly it dawned on her that no longer were they coupled, that he was sprawled back in the driving seat, breathing heavily as though he had undergone a terrific physical strain. She moved, her thighs caught against something hard that clicked, creaked. The door handle, the door was swinging back on its hinges, the fog coming in at her in wisps of icy vapor.

Impulsively, instinctively, she jumped backward, felt mud beneath her feet and wan moonlight eerily penetrating the dense fog.

"Hey, what the hell d'you think you're doing?" A yell of rage from the car, strangely muffled.

Thelma Brown broke into a blind run, heedless of direction, only one thought in her mind and that was to get as far away as possible from the man who had done this to her. He might even kill her if he caught her.

She was aware of thick mire and splashing water, rushes that stood vertically like inverted assegais, mist that blotted out her surroundings. Trees that sprouted grotesquely, multiarmed ogres trying to bar her way as she ran between them, plucking at her, scraping her naked flesh.

Panicking, running until she could run no more, lying

beneath one of the stunted trees and trying to listen above the noise of her thumping heart. A movement to her left as though somebody threshed blindly in a deep bog? She could not be sure.

Distant thunder . . . no, it was continuous, not the right volume, more like a series of explosions that went on and on. And on. The moon was brighter, casting weird shadows, yet again the light was not right, instead of silvery it was orange-tinted like the reflection of leaping flames or a stormy sunset.

Staring skyward she had the impression that the sun was rising, spreading an aura of fire across the whole sky behind a smoky haze. Cowering, not wanting to look any more but knowing that she had to, a kind of hypnotism.

And then, louder by the second, she heard the sound of an approaching aircraft, a heavy lumbering mechanical bird that vibrated the air until it was painful to the ears.

SEVEN

Andy Dark saw the rowing boat looming up out of the mist, its bows now only a few yards from the marshy shore. He stared, tried to make out what was happening through a curtain of swirling gray vapor.

The boat grated on the bottom and a man leaped ashore, struggled to pull the cumbersome craft farther up the beach; the others (there appeared to be four of them) threw a length of rope which he fastened to an old tree stump. They were all leaping out, talking in low voices, splashing to and fro in the water as they began unloading boxes, wooden crates which they supported on their shoulders with difficulty, stacking them on the soft grass, talking in low muttered voices, glancing furtively about them the whole time.

Andy counted three men and a boy who could not have been more than thirteen, moving, bustling outlines, details hidden by the fog. And only yards away those men in their strange attire, their three-cornered hats pulled down over their faces, watched and waited. Deathly cold, not a breath of wind now, the light beginning to fail.

Andy Dark wished again that he had his watch; surely it could not be late afternoon already. He had the feeling that time was a commodity that existed only in irrational fragments in this place. These terrible mists were responsible for it in some inexplicable way. Suddenly the Droy legends were no longer wild tales to be dismissed lightly.

Andy crept forward another few yards, crouched down again behind a tussock of reeds. Now he could see the newcomers more clearly and his mouth went dry. Ragged clothing that had no place in the twentieth century outside museums or theatrical costumiers, patched coats and rough homespun shirts, breeches rolled up above the knees, wading barefooted in the water. Bearded features except for the boy who was emaciated, terrible to behold. Some disease, it could not be anything else, had eaten into the flesh on his face, a spreading malignant rash that exposed the bone in places. Barely able to lift the boxes yet struggling to do so as though he was afraid of what might happen to him if he shirked; cringing every time one of the others spoke to him. Gruff whispers which the fog seemed to magnify. Hurrying, all of them glancing about them fearfully, an obvious furtiveness, a haste to be finished and away.

Andy's flesh crept. Smugglers without a doubt yet this was no highly organized trafficking. Had there been a motor launch moored close by, even a conventional boat of some kind, he could have accepted the situation. But this was like some dreadful nightmare, the product of a fevered brain.

Suddenly the hidden men leaped into action, on their feet and cutting off the smugglers' retreat back to their boat. A scream; Andy thought it came from the boy. Shouts, curses. A muffled explosion; somebody had fired a pistol but the bullet appeared to have missed. A melee, struggling, fighting. The ambushers were armed with clubs, crude staves into which nails had been hammered, the points protruding wickedly.

A blow, one of the smugglers dropped and Andy saw the gaping head wound, a deep gash that split right into the skull, splintering the bone . . . Another was bent double, clutching at his groin, the third being held, screaming as his captors broke his legs with their cudgels. Brutal mutilation, and then came a realization which had Andy wanting to burst into headlong panicstricken flight. *There was no blood, not a single trickle of sticky scarlet fluid from any one of the multitude of wounds!*

Yet the sheer awfulness of the encounter held the conservation officer spellbound. These savage brutes who were undoubtedly some kind of Customs officers had turned on the boy. Two of them held him while a third raised a nail-spiked club. Andy's instinct was to rush to the other's aid. He could not stand by and witness a cowardly murder, but his legs refused to move. Whatever his feelings he was forced to watch, not even able to turn his head away, screaming mutely. For Christ's *sake,* you *can't!*

They had forced the boy's mouth open, were jamming the head of a narrow cudgel between the stretched lips, the rusted nails ripping the flesh, gouging and tearing at the skin. Twisting, pushing, muffling the cries of agony, shredding gums and tongue, raking the back of the throat, clawing for the tonsils. Withdrawing, a tongueless child mouthing silent pleas for mercy. *But still there was no blood!*

They had his arms pinioned behind him and were frog-marching him along with the other two smugglers; coming inshore—toward Andy Dark! And still Andy was struggling to move, transfixed like a wedding guest beholding the Ancient Mariner. Eddying fog, a breeze coming in off the sea, the mist no longer adequate cover for the lurking watcher.

Shouts, they had seen him. A pistol exploded with a dull boom and he heard the whistle of a spherical ball of lead passing a yard or so above his head. Fighting with his limbs, his brain, yelling at them to coordinate. And then movement returned to his aching muscles, arthritic joints creaking, stretching. Extricating himself from the mud into which his feet had sunk, those figures only yards behind him now, gaining on him.

Running, the wood ahead of him, he'd have to go through it whether he liked it or not, try and lose his pursuers in there. Swirling mist; it might clear altogether or else it might come down thicker than ever. He could hear their wheezing breaths behind him, feet that seemed to move faster than his own. If only he could have had a start on them he was sure he would have outdistanced them. Nightmare thoughts about what would happen to him if they caught him, those devilish cudgels with their pincushions of rusty nails, the way they had ripped out that young boy's mouth. Clubbed to death, a score of atrocities from these torturers from a bygone century might be his fate.

Andy's lungs hurt, he tasted the sour odor of the mist, its stagnant marsh gases which constricted his breathing. These men were some kind of apparition, he tried to tell himself, an astral projection with the fog acting as a screen on which to show the film, scenes long dead, perhaps some kind of embodiment of vibration. They couldn't hurt him, they could only harm their own kind.

They were gaining on him fast. Another shot, another bullet cutting through the air above his head, the feeling that they did not want to shoot him—they wanted him alive for some diabolical reason. If only he could reach the wood . . .

And then he fell. He wasn't sure whether he had tripped over a tussock of grass or whether his legs had finally given out. Momentary blackness, fainting for a split second and then the deluge of stinking black water revived him. Lying there, lifting his head so that he did not drown in the shallow pool, closing his eyes. Anticipating a pistol ball splintering his skull. One brief moment of pain, no more. He had read somewhere that you never heard the shot that got you. Silence, just an awareness that they were clustered around him. Wincing, bracing himself for the shattering impact of one of those clubs, being battered mercilessly to death.

Hands seized him, dragged him to his knees, a blow from a fist jerking his head back, looking up into those features which might have belonged to freshly exhumed corpses. Eyes that stared unflickeringly, mouths that were twisted cavities of hatred, foul breath mingling with the stink of the fog.

They exchanged glances, muttered in a dialect which he barely understood, a kind of mongrel English. "Another smuggler hid'n on merse . . . take 'un to dungeons . . ."

Andy was hauled to his feet, strong fingers gripping both wrists, and even as they pushed him forward he was frighteningly aware of the coldness of the hands which held him. *No way could the temperature of any human being drop so low and life still course through the body!*

He stumbled, almost fell, and a booted foot kicked him on the thigh. All around him feet squelched in the marsh grass and reeds, and somewhere somebody was whimpering. It had to be the boy, probably the other two smugglers were being dragged along too, taken to those dungeons . . . Anger penetrated his fear. I'm not a smuggler, I'm not interested in your quarrel with these men. But there was no way he was going to be allowed to prove his innocence or even state his case. These Customs officers, for surely they could not be anything else, were judge and jury in their own primitive age.

The mist had begun to thicken again by the time they reached the wood. One of the captors went on ahead, the party converging into almost single file in his wake, a route that threaded its way through the trees, detoured deep reedy bogs, at times seeming to cut back on itself, until eventually the outline of a large turreted building loomed out of the fog. Droy House, without a doubt, Andy decided—as it once used to be.

Centuries before it had been a castle, probably partly demolished in the Civil War and then rebuilt. Gaunt and sinister, towering over the treetops, the main entrance gates wide open like some monster preparing to swallow its prey.

Andy's legs threatened to buckle under him again but there was to be no respite. Up a flight of moss-covered stone steps and into a hallway that had once perhaps formed part of the courtyard. Wooden paneling faced part of the interior stone wall, a table and chair set in the center but no other item of furniture was visible. At the far end a trap door stood open, below which yawned a black square with steps going down into the darkness.

Andy Dark's captors released him, gave him a push which almost sent him headlong down that stone stairway. There was no mistaking his fate, no way he could protest. Holding on to the wall for support, feeling his way, hearing the other prisoners following him. The boy was gurgling, trying to scream but only succeeding in making animallike noises, grunts and whimpers. The injured man, unable to stand, fell; crawled. Suddenly one of the smugglers, the last one down the steps shouted, "For mercy's sake, no. Not in here! Never again shall we see the light o' day!"

Somebody up above laughed and a sudden fierce heavy thud which had an air of finality about it extinguished that single square of gray light, turned it to pitch darkness. Cries of hopelessness, the boy whimpering again in his own tongueless manner.

Andy moved forward, feeling his way with outstretched arms, following the wall. They seemed to be in some kind of passage that led on into the bowels of Droy House; testing each step, a fear lest some deep pit might lie ahead of him and all the time aware of the pathetic yet terrible creatures bringing up the rear. Mentally hurrying, fearing lest an icy cold hand might seize him, pull him back. Starting to panic as an awful realization dawned on him: life sentence. *"And life shall mean life."* Here forever, starving, dying of thirst . . . eventually becoming one of *them!*

He could hear the others floundering about in the darkness. Somebody fell, cursed in a strange dialect. Gruff reprimands, probably aimed at the boy. They all seemed oblivious of the fact that a stranger had been imprisoned with them but sooner or later they must become aware of that fact.

Hunger did terrible things to civilized Man, Andy had read something only comparatively recently; plane-crash victims who had feasted on the dead. He tasted bile in his throat, his stomach rejecting the idea instantly, wanting to vomit at the thought of . . . of *those* things, their putrified flesh.

Rats . . . he could hear them scurrying. In a way they seemed friendly creatures compared with those with which he had been entombed in this damp airless place. A fluttering somewhere close by and he recognized the wingbeats of bats. The fact that bats inhabited this place meant that they had to be able to get in and out, probably only a tiny niche somewhere but in this kind of situation you found yourself clutching at straws, building up hopes only to have them dashed but knowing that without them you would give up and die.

He had always had a secret fear of underground places and now they were manifesting themselves into awful reality. Cobwebs touched him, had him clawing at them. If he wasn't already mad then he surely would be soon. Listening, holding his breath. He could not hear the others, not even the sound of faint breathing. Perhaps they hadn't been here at all, he had imagined it. Or else they had died; no that couldn't happen because they were already dead, they had to be.

Fearful lest they were stalking him, ravenous beasts who smelled fresh meat and were determined not to starve. Glancing about him, seeing nothing except total blackness. He stretched out his hands again, determined to explore this place, to find out where the bats came and went.

Then suddenly he touched something; recognized it instantly as soft human flesh, warm and living; moving, tensing. A body hanging from the wall that screamed deafeningly and screamed again!

Andy Dark jerked back, stumbled, was on the verge of blind flight, saw in his mind his wretched companions again. But their flesh was cold and dead even though they moved and spoke. It was not one of them, it was somebody else who like himself had been captured and thrown down here.

"Who . . . is it?" his whisper echoed and reechoed. *"Who is it? Who . . . is . . . it?"*

Who? Waiting for an answer, hearing the other's sharp intake of breath as though in preparation for another scream. And then came one word, a name, uttered in fear and hope, disbelief. The old game of building up hopes and having them dashed. A name. His own.

"Andy?" Fearful female tones, barely recognizable but enough for him to know.

"Carol!" Oh Jesus God, what have they done to you, my darling?

He rushed forward, felt at the pinioned body. It was female, naked and very real, sagging in its manacles. How? Why? When? Questions that could be answered later: first he had to free Carol Embleton.

"I'll get you out of whatever this contraption is." He slid his hand up one of her arms, located the iron bracelet. A sudden fear that it might be locked, the key taken away by those diabolical jailers. Then he sighed his relief aloud; a crude clasp, nothing more. Rusted and stiff, he prised at it, felt it creak open reluctantly. The other arm, the ankles, Carol tumbling on to him, crying, still not believing. "Oh, Andy, is it *really* you?"

"It is," he said, holding her close and kissing her, staring into the Stygian darkness again, fearful lest at any moment those terrible beings might suddenly grab at them with cold, dead hands. But they didn't, there was no sound. They might never have existed.

"It's madness all this," he said, speaking in a low whisper. "It seems the old legends have some truth in them after all. Smugglers, Customs officers from the eighteenth century, ghouls who once walked the mists of Droy Wood and its adjoining marshlands. It was the mist that was responsible for all these happenings."

"Whatever are you talking about?" She clutched at his arm. "You're talking in riddles, Andy. I never saw any Customs officers. It was the German pilot who imprisoned me here."

"A German pilot!"

"That's right. After I fled from this man James Foster it was like the whole sky was ablaze. There was bombing and firing and then this plane crash. A German plane but the pilot managed to bail out. He claims that the war isn't over yet, that Britain is tottering on the brink of defeat. He locked me up for the Gestapo to deal with me when the Nazis overrun Britain."

"Christ Alive!" Andy Dark's brain reeled with this latest piece of information. "Right now we're locked in ancient dungeons, there's a Nazi and a sex maniac at large, not to mention a gang of ghoulish things prowling about with cudgels spiked with nails!"

"Oh, what's it all mean, Andy?" Carol Embleton's whole body was shaking. She couldn't take much more.

"I don't know," he confessed. "Only that the mists that blanket the wood and the marsh from time to time are responsible, somehow having retained past evils, kept them alive. Like those old films they keep showing on the television from time to time. I guess the dead live on here, ensnaring any who get caught up in the wood in the fogs. Like a sort of time machine. I can't offer any other explanation."

"It's ghastly." She didn't want to go into details of her encounter with Foster, that could all come later.

"We've got to get out of here," he muttered. "We'll try the trap door first. Maybe I can smash a way through it. Now, hold on to me and we'll try and find our way back to the entrance."

Once again Andy Dark led the way, one arm at full stretch in front of him, the other holding Carol's hand, feeling his way along the damp mossy wall, testing each step before putting his full weight on it. Tense, skin prickling all the while, afraid that at any second an icy hand would reach out and grab him, or he would hear that boy whimpering with pain, trying to scream with his lacerated mouth from which no blood poured. But there was no sign, no sound of anybody.

"Here are the steps," he said with hope in his voice, fearful lest the Droy curse might bring them another terrible phase from its evil past. One at a time up the steps until he touched the trap door, felt its studded iron bands and his hopes began to fade. So heavy, so strong, a square of reinforced seasoned oak which had probably withstood the frenzied onslaughts of scores of prisoners over the centuries. "I'll have to find something to smash it with." And that meant going back down to the dungeon, groping around in the pitch blackness. He should have thought of it in the first place.

His hands explored the trap door, pushed upward, and felt it move. Those rusty hinges squealed, a crack of gray daylight appeared. Heaving, afraid that he was mistaken, that it was some kind of cruel trick designed to demoralize the damned. Another six inches, the hinged door lifting, finally thudding back against the stone wall of the hallway.

"I can't believe it." He still didn't, hauling Carol up behind him, both of them scrambling out of that evil-smelling hole in case at any second the trap door decided to slam back shut. "It wasn't even bolted! We're out, girl, my God, we're out!"

They crouched there blinking in the faint daylight; it might have been dawn, dusk, any time of day. Winter daylight, darkened by the presence of a thick fog outside.

"We'd better get back to the road," Carol found herself whispering. "It can't be far."

"No, I'm sure it isn't." He licked his lips, remembered only too well what it was like out there, the same as it had been for centuries, a dark stunted wood where the foul marshes had infiltrated, where people got lost and were never heard of again. "We'd better make a move. Here," he said, slipping off his muddy thornproof jacket, "put this around you. Now, we'll go as fast as we can, take a direct line." *And I hope to God we're going in the right direction.*

They had barely taken a half-dozen steps across the stone-flagged hall, when they heard footsteps coming from the balcony above, the slow, measured footfalls of hard leather soles, something eerily positive about them.

"There's . . . somebody coming down the stairs." Carol Embleton clutched at him, dared not look, felt him whirling around, heard his gasp of fear and amazement.

Halfway down the stairs the tall figure, clad in an immaculate gray-green uniform, the tunic unbuttoned, stood watching them with cold unblinking pale blue eyes. And in his hand, held almost casually, the barrel trained unwaveringly on them, was a Luger automatic pistol.

"So," Bertie Hass smiled but there was no humor in the stretching of his thin lips, "you think you can escape from *my* castle, eh! My friends, I think that it would be easier for you to escape from Colditz!"

The German began a slow descent, laughed gloatingly. "Consider yourselves prisoners of war, caught in the act of trying to escape and for that there is only one penalty!"

EIGHT

Reluctantly James Foster had abandoned his search for Carol Embleton. Several times he had heard her splashing on ahead of him through the dense reed-beds, was confident that he would overtake her. So he would have done had it not been for this damnable fog. Now she was lost and he had to face up to the fact that so was he. He had lost all sense of direction.

His priority was a reasonably dry place in which to pass the rest of the night; once daylight came he would soon catch her. He shivered with cold, eventually located a large alder tree growing out of a hummock of ground above the level of the marsh. He settled himself down and once his anger had simmered he began to feel drowsy, almost relaxed.

He would kill her, he had to. He would never forget the sheer thrill of his last killing, that tall dark-haired girl who had eventually given up her struggles and let him do what he wanted. As his orgasm mounted his hands had encircled her throat, begun to squeeze. It had made her thresh beautifully beneath him, her death throes in time with his own thrustings. He had ejaculated and she had died, a perfect combination. He did not regret it one little bit. It had served to whet his appetite for another killing.

Had Carol not been riding him then she would have died the same way. Damn the cow, he had intended to screw her a second time and throttle her at the very peak of his orgasm but she had jumped and run. Which was why they were both spending the night in this damn awful place.

Just thinking about her gave him another erection. Tomorrow he would find her, fuck her, and kill her. That was a foregone conclusion. He . . .

Something had him opening his eyes, staring up at the sky in bewilderment. There was a fire somewhere, a big one that lit up the heavens. Explosions, firing, the sound of aircraft whining and droning. He sat up.

And then he saw the blazing bomber, watched it fall like a stone out of the sky, explode somewhere not far away with a force that vibrated the ground. In the ethereal reflection of the blazing aircraft he saw the parachutist gliding down, decided that he had better go and investigate.

Hell, he should have minded his own bleeding business. Now he was floundering in this bloody morass again, looking for another dry place to pass the night for he had not located the man who had parachuted down and he would never find that patch of higher ground beneath the alder again.

Then, unbelievably, he chanced upon a stretch of almost dry ground beneath some taller oaks, trod his way through a carpet of dead leaves and ferns that were brittle beneath his feet. The rain had stopped and for a moment the moon shone down brightly through the entwining branches. A little way ahead of him he could make out a clearing, an area where it was almost as light as day.

He walked on forward, emerged into the clearing, and suddenly became uneasily aware that he wasn't alone, felt the presence of others before he saw the shadowy shapes grouped around the clearing in a circle, some of them having moved so that they ringed him completely.

Fear, searching for a gap in the circle through which to

make a run for it but there was none. Staring from one cowled figure to the next, trying to count them and losing count; there were dozens of them!

"Who are you?" Jesus, they gave him the creeps just standing there looking at him, pairs of eyes that seemed to glow balefully in the moonlight like a pack of wolves that had crept up and surrounded an unwary traveler. "I said who the fuck are you? Are you dumb or something?"

As though at some prearranged signal the watchers began to converge on him, the circle diminishing, crowding him. He backed away, turned one way then the other. He wanted to scream. Suddenly they halted and a tall cloaked figure, his face shadowed by his voluminous cowl, detached himself from the rest and stepped forward a few paces.

"We were expecting you," he said, his voice deep and resonant. "For we are the Oke Priests who rule this place and you have dared to trespass in our domain. However, we have need of you. We knew you would come, that the old ones would not forsake us. But there is plenty of time . . ."

You're fucking nutters, James Foster thought, swallowed. Suddenly he was very cold, shivering uncontrollably, felt an urge to urinate, to empty his bowels. This lot were up to something, playing at black magic or some other kind of cult rites. He'd read about them in the papers, how they desecrated churchyards, sometimes dug up bodies. Ugh!

"Look," he began, self-consciously because he was stark naked, standing there with his hands folded across his genitals like an erring schoolboy facing his headmaster, "I don't want to interrupt your, er . . . meeting . . . I'll be on my way, leave you to it."

Foster had barely taken a couple of steps before he was seized from behind, his attackers moving with unbelievable stealth and speed, cold hands grabbing him, hurting him. He screamed, struggled, felt himself being lifted aloft, carried; laid flat on his back on a rough cold surface. A flat rock of some kind, rough so that it grazed his skin. Staring up into faces that were still bathed in shadow, only those terrible eyes visible.

He ceased struggling because it was futile; even when they brought ropes and began to bind him tightly; arms, legs, pinioning him to the slab across his chest, the only movement remaining to him a slight raising of the neck. He could lift his head a few inches but it was painful, pulled on his spine.

"What's . . . the idea?" he said, not really wanting to know.

"The old ones are becoming impatient." A flat intonation. "It is a long time since we offered them a sacrifice but now we can make amends. We now await the rising of the sun. Lie still and repent whilst there is still time."

Silence. If they had cursed him, threatened him with terrible atrocities it would have been better than this awful stillness.

They had moved back into the shadows where he could not see them any longer. They might even have left except that he sensed their presence, felt their eyes feasting on his nakedness. *Repent whilst there is still time.* James Foster knew that he was going to die.

For a time his brain seemed dulled as though he had taken some stupefying drug, an anesthetic. The lust and the anger in him were dead, a kind of purification of his brain which allowed him to see things in perspective; his own role that of a spectator. The girl, Carol, she was somewhere out here in these woods, lost and frightened.

Because of himself. These druids, for surely that was what they were, might find her. And if they did . . . guilt, fear. *His* fault. He must not tell them about her. Lie if they asked him.

Torture of a kind he had never experienced before in his life as though he were being forced to search his own mind, tell *them* what they wanted to know although they probably knew it already. He could feel their power, sucking it out of him like some heavy-duty industrial vacuum cleaner. Confess, for time is running out. Cleanse yourself.

Don't tell them about the girl in case they go looking for her. They already know. I liked her, I didn't *want* to hurt her, just couldn't help myself. She wouldn't have gone with me if I hadn't made her, and I'd've killed her afterward so that nobody else could have her, so that she didn't go back to that boyfriend of hers. You bastard! I wish I could tell her I'm sorry. Oh God, if I could only see her for a couple of minutes to tell her. But it's too late; she'll hate you for the rest of her life.

The one you killed . . . he tried to push the recollection from him but it wouldn't go. She had tried to plead but tightening fingers on her throat had garrotted the words. He hadn't felt any remorse then but he did now. I want to die so that I don't have to think about it anymore but if the police catch me they won't kill me because there isn't a death penalty. Everybody wants the death sentence brought back because it's merciful, puts you out of your misery. Instead they shut you away and you go crazy reliving every second.

You'll die, all right, but you won't forget because here the dead live on, forced to relive their actions for eternity.

Remember the first time you ever did anything, the strange thrill you got? You were seventeen at the time.

Don't remind me about it. You will recall every second of it. Foster squirmed, these bastards were really scouring him out now. Confess, it isn't long until sunrise.

I tried to date Beth. She was only fifteen but her folks poisoned her mind against me. You're a virgin, Beth, and you'll stay that way until your wedding night, and you won't be marrying *him.* You can tell by the expression in those eyes of his what *he* wants. We forbid you to see him.

So James Foster had waylaid Beth on her way home from school with all the precision of a carefully planned military operation. He'd followed her, found out the route she took when she got off the school bus, a shortcut across the fields to the council estate. Small and slim, mousy-colored hair, but well developed for her age. Masturbating night after night just thinking about her. She had become an obsession. And then he had struck.

She had backed away, given a little cry of fear when he had emerged from the bushes to bar her path. She saw the bulge in the front of his trousers and it frightened her like the look in his eyes did. You're a virgin aren't you, Beth? I hate virgins. So frightened she had stepped back into the bushes with him, trembling as he undid her clothing. No, I'm not going to fuck you, I just want to look. And to feel. Tender young breasts, a sparse growth of pubic hair, exciting him as he had never been excited before. Fingering her so that she began to cry . . . You wouldn't even date me now Beth if your folks said it was okay, would you? It's *their* fault that I've had to do this to you. But before I let you go there's something I want to show you!

She hadn't wanted to look, had turned her head away so that he had had to grab her by those soft wavy locks and make her watch. I'll bet you've never even seen one of these before, Beth. Well, you have now and if you take your eyes off it once I'll get really angry so that no boy will ever want to date you again with a face like you'll have. Now watch, you virgin bitch!

She had watched, trembling violently with fear and revulsion. He had shuddered, gasping for breath. No, I'm not going to fuck you because I want you to spend months, years, just thinking what it *might* be like. Get me? You'll never forget this as long as you live.

She had sobbed but dared not close her eyes, watched until he was satisfied, writhed as his warmth spurted on her bare stomach and thighs as though it scalded her. And then he'd left, running breathlessly, knowing that she would not tell what had happened to her. She would never tell anybody.

She hadn't told. A month later they had found her body in the river and that had given him one helluva thrill. No guilt—until now! You killed her, James Foster, as surely as you murdered that other girl whose name you never found out.

I want to die. You'll die all right but there will be no escape in death. Life means life—even in death!

It was getting lighter now, the waning moonlight merging with a grayness that was not wholly the Droy mist. Creeping daylight, cold and penetrating. Foster lifted his head slightly, saw the figures moving forward. One of them, taller than the rest, had thrown back his cowl and had replaced it with some kind of crude cap made from animal hides, possibly a fox. He saw the other's features, wanted to jerk his head away but could not. Skin stretched across high cheekbones like ancient parchment, eyes hooded so that you could not see them; they might have been empty sockets. Almost lipless, just a single blackened tooth that appeared to be loose, might fall out at any second. Yet his movements were swift and sure, almost agile as he advanced on the trussed man.

"It is nearly time." A lisp, spittle stringing from his mouth. "The new day is here and soon the sun will rise. The first ray will strike this stone, bathe you in its glory . . ."

"Hold on." Foster felt the panic coming back again as he noticed for the first time the long-bladed knife which the other was holding, steel that was dulled brown as though with rust. Except that he knew that it was not rust. "You can't do this . . ."

"The old ones will not wait." A recitation as though these were oft-repeated words. "We have not forgotten them, how they have preserved us here over the centuries, enabled us to live when others have died and their bones have rotted. The mists are sent to protect us, to hide us from those who would destroy us and our ancient place of worship."

"You can't kill me," Foster screamed, straining at his bonds. "It's . . . *murder!*"

"Which is why those who sit in judgment beyond the mists have sent you here." Those eyes seemed to glow redly for a second or two. "You have murdered in a world where the penalty is not severe enough. This council has passed the sentence of death on you but it will not be oblivion, for after death there is life in many forms. You will live on here in this ancient place, in a torment undreamed of, for eternity. You will murder again, pay the supreme price many times over, because it has been ordained so."

Foster lay back, closed his eyes, knew that the tall one spoke the truth.

"Look!" A shout that precipitated the beginning of a

weird monotone chanting like the wind rustling the thick reed-beds, growing louder and louder.

The sky was tinted pink, a roseate hue, the fog swirling, clearing to make way for it as though some mighty force was rising out of the wood and dispersing it. Cold; James Foster shivered for with the coming of day this could no longer be dismissed as some dreadful nightmare. It was reality in the sober atmosphere of daylight.

The chanting rose to a pitch, the throng closer now, grouped around the huge sacrificial stone, watching the sky. And Foster's guilt, his remorse, had evaporated along with the darkness. He did not want to die like this.

"Stop it, you bastards!" he screamed, strained at the ropes. "You've had your fun. This is murder. You'll be put away for it. Let me go, d'you hear? *For fuck's sake let me go!*"

"The sentence has been passed." The tall druid bent over him, the blade only inches away from the rapist's throat. "The old ones will command us to carry it out. We cannot disobey them."

A hush. Any second now, the pink clouds overhead changing to a deep red, the lower ones having dispersed as though in readiness for the rising of the sun, clearing a path so that its first rays should not be obstructed. Foster caught a glimpse of some of the faces beneath the cowls, now no longer hidden by the shadows, and closed his eyes to shut them out. God Almighty, the dead had surely risen in Droy Wood.

A cry of jubilation in unison, a bowing of heads; a blood-red ray of sunlight hit the oblong stone with the suddenness of a torch switched on in the darkness, bathed the head and shoulders of the naked victim, seemed to focus on the throat.

One swift movement from the Oke Priest with all the

expertise of an executioner who has inherited all the skills of his trade. Striking, gashing, stepping back in time to avoid the jet of scarlet which spouted high into the air, a claret fountain spurting and splattering, the agonized terrified face of the offered sacrifice awash with his own blood. Writhing within the confines of his bonds, gurgling his last because he could not scream. Shuddering, twitching.

Dying.

The old priest knelt and the others followed suit, their incantations whispered now for they were truly afraid of the old gods. Sacrifices were demanded but it was not always easy in a place where only the dead walked. A chance traveler sometimes but this place was a jungle, numerous dead from past centuries hunting living prey. The mists controlled their fate, brought back times long gone, chose the time according to their moods. All of them remembered that one who had floated down from the burning skies that night like some gigantic bird, how they had hunted him through the reed-beds, almost lost him to the ghouls with the triangular hats. The man had all the cunning of a wild beast but in the end they had run him down, claimed him for their own. He was one of them, now, just as this one would be, a soul in torment, a slave of the Oke Priests.

For the old religion ruled this place and their slaves did their bidding. The gods were demanding more sacrifices; they had been kept waiting too long. Every killing in this place was done in their name.

NINE

Thelma Brown awoke stiff and cold, stared into the thickening mist. It had still not cleared but at least it was daylight. She shivered with the cold, stood up and moved about in an attempt to get warm, get her cramped muscles working again.

It was awful, unbelievable what had happened last night. I'm sorry Mum, John, you were right after all, I shouldn't have gone, it was dangerous. That man who picked me up couldn't have been a policeman, he wouldn't have acted like that if he was. But where were the police, why didn't they come looking for her? As soon as it got light enough they would be sure to search the wood again and then they would find her. But in the meantime the man who had raped her was still in the wood. It had to be the man named Foster, the one who had abducted Carol Embleton, probably killed Andy Dark, because it couldn't be anybody else. He must have left the wood, picked up another car and driven that same road again ahead of the policeman who was going to pick up Thelma, beaten him to it, taken advantage of the fog. Damn the fog, it was responsible for everything that had happened last night.

She felt sick, a combination of fear, cold and hunger leading to nausea. Perhaps she could find her way back to the road, it couldn't be all that far. Take a straight line in . . . she didn't know which direction. Everywhere looked the same in here, dead or dying twisted oaks, bogs and thick reeds. And the awful silence, not even a crow calling raucously. But she couldn't just stop because she might still be here when darkness fell again. Don't panic, they'll find you; they'll have to or else there'll be a public outcry. POLICE DECOY SNATCHED BY RAPIST. JAMES FOSTER STILL AT LARGE. They would move heaven and earth to find her.

She saw what appeared to be a well-trodden muddy path leading away through the trees, skirting some tall reeds, decided at once that she would follow it. She trod cautiously, fearfully. The rushes were tall and thick, could have concealed an army. She kept as far from them as the path would allow, started, almost screamed once, when they rustled as though somebody lurked in there waiting to spring out at her. It could not have been the wind because there wasn't any, not so much as a faint breeze. And the mist seemed to be thickening all the time. You'll never leave here, Thelma Brown. *Nobody leaves Droy Wood when the mists cover it.*

The path snaked on and on. She wondered who had made it, an uneasy thought. No cattle or sheep came in here; wild animals then, foxes, badgers, rabbits traveling constantly to and fro through the night hours. She tried to convince herself that it was the creatures of the wild, might have done so had it not been for the total silence around her, a dead place which even the birds and animals shunned.

The path was cutting away to her left now, winding through the trees, going on and on, visibility down to less than ten yards. Thelma could not get that fiery sky out of her mind, that blazing aircraft, the parachutist. It had seemed so real at the time but it had to be a hallucination because it couldn't possibly have been real. The human brain played strange tricks on one when under stress.

She stopped, listened again. If only she could pick up the sound of a passing car or lorry, know that the road was not far away, that she was going in the right direction. But always there was just the silence.

The ground beneath her feet was drier now, leaves rustling as her bare feet scuffed through them. The trees, too, mostly oaks, retained a vestige of browning greenery as though they had not surrendered completely to this place where everything died. Hope, hurrying. If only that man Foster had not been in the vicinity she would have yelled for help; the police must be starting to search for her by now.

And then she came upon the young girl, not much older than ten or eleven. Thelma started, thought it must be another trick her confused mind was playing on her. She stared, saw the child sitting on a dead tree trunk watching her, smiling, not in the least bit surprised. Long golden hair done up into pigtails, her head seemingly too large for her slender young body; pretty, wide blue eyes, a flowery blue dress that fell to the ankles of her bare legs. Quaint, old-fashioned, Thelma thought, just how Mum might have looked when she was young. Or even Grandma.

The child did not appear to be in the least frightened or concerned, holding some reeds which she had been attempting to plait, playing idly just as she might have done in the meadows on a hot summer's day.

"Hallo," she said, still smiling, "fancy seeing you here."

"Fancy seeing *you* here," Thelma echoed, and for some reason another shudder ran over her body. "Aren't you cold with just a summer dress on?"

"*You* haven't got *any* clothes on." Almost a prudish accusation.

"No . . . no, I haven't, have I?" Thelma glanced down at herself, experienced an unfamiliar embarrassment.

"Why haven't you?" Wide questioning eyes demanding an explanation.

"Because . . ."—I can't tell her I've been raped, and neither must I let her go wandering off on her own with *him* about—"because I fell in the mud and my clothes got all wet and muddy so there wasn't much point in wearing them. I hung them on a tree."

"My mummy used to say that you only wore clothes to stop other people from looking at your body, that we didn't really need them. She's dead now, though."

"Oh, I'm sorry." Poor kid.

"I'm sorry, too. But would you like to see my daddy?"

"Oh, yes . . . but I can't . . . like *this.*"

"He won't mind."

Thelma knew she was blushing yet the spark of hope within her that had almost gone out was glowing again. A child and her father, they had to know the way out of Droy Wood. It was funny that she did not recognize the girl, though. She knew most of the locals but this one was a stranger to her. They were building some new houses just outside the village, though, on the city side. Perhaps she came from one of those. She had to because no local would go anywhere near the wood, particularly when the mist covered it.

"My daddy's back there," she said pointing vaguely behind her. "It's quite a way, it'll take us ten minutes to walk it."

"That's okay. What's your name?"

"Elsie."

"That's nice." It's old-fashioned, too. People don't use names like that these days. Still, what's in a name?

"Come on then." Elsie stretched out a hand.

Thelma took it, felt icy cold fingers entwining with her own, transmitting a shiver. The child was deathly cold. "You're cold. You ought to wear more clothes or else you'll be catching your . . . *(death)* . . . you'll be catching pneumonia."

"I'm all right, I'm used to it." Her voice was husky, almost as though she had a sore throat. "It's not really cold, it's just the damp fog."

Elsie was pulling on Thelma's hand, overtaking her as though there were some sudden hurry.

"What's your daddy doing in the wood?" Serve me right if she told me to mind my own damned business.

A pause, clearing her throat. "He's always in the wood these days. You'll see for yourself soon, though."

They walked on in silence, a slight uneasiness creeping between them.

"I miss my mummy." A note of sadness, almost a sob. "I loved her."

"How long's she . . ."

"A few days. Would you like to see her grave?"

No, I wouldn't. "Sometime perhaps but hadn't we better go and meet your daddy first?"

"I suppose so."

The other's mood had changed; sullen, those cold fingers detaching themselves from Thelma's, walking faster, striding on ahead.

The wood was not quite so boggy here, the ground a thick carpet of dead leaves which had gathered over the years, the permanent smell of decay almost overpowering. A wide space, perhaps the trees here had been felled at some time or other or else they had just blown down and rotted. Ahead of her Thelma saw what appeared to be a huge circular hole in the ground, a pit of some kind that had once been dug out manually because there was a large mound on the opposite side. It grew weeds and moss so the excavation had been a very long time ago. She wondered what on earth anybody would want to dig here for.

"They used to get peat from here a long time ago, when my daddy was a little boy." Elsie appeared to have the uncanny knack of being able to read your thoughts. If her father had been here as a boy then they couldn't live in those new houses.

"You live around here then?" A direct question; perhaps too direct.

"Sort of."

What's your other name? What's your daddy do for a living? And just *where* do you live? Thelma checked her curiosity. She would find out soon enough.

"My daddy's down there." Elsie had run on ahead, was standing looking down into the deep hole.

Thelma halted, a sudden inexplicable terror gripping her, a tremor in her voice when she spoke. "Whatever do you mean . . . *down there?*"

"Down *there!*" Impatience, a tiny finger stabbing down at the hole. "If you don't believe me come and look for yourself. I thought you wanted to meet him. I've brought you specially."

"All . . . right." Thelma Brown's legs felt suddenly rubbery. Perhaps it was some kind of joke, this child was funny in the head. Her father wasn't here at all except in her own imagination. It was all a game of pretense, she had run away from home, dodged school and come to indulge in her own make-believe games in Droy Wood. Her mother wasn't dead, just morbid childhood fantasy. They might be, probably were, searching for her at this

very moment. CHILD GOES MISSING IN DROY WOOD. SEX
KILLER STILL AT LARGE. MASSIVE POLICE HUNT.

"All right, I'll come and meet your daddy." Better
humor her for the moment and then I'll grab hold of her
and I won't let her go until the police arrive. *If they
arrive.*

Cautiously Thelma approached the edge of the pit. It
was deep, she couldn't see the bottom yet. Sheer sides of
thick black mud. Possibly it was a peat excavation after
all but how the hell did diggers get up and down without
a ladder? There certainly wasn't a ladder in sight now.
No, her father couldn't possibly be down there. Pretend
for the moment that he is, though.

Mentally measuring the depth as she saw more and
more of those steep sides. Ten . . . eleven . . . twelve
feet and we haven't reached the bottom yet. Fifteen . . .
black brackish water in the bottom because this whole
place was nothing more than a wooded marsh that eventually the sea would erode and reclaim.

She could see the bottom all right now, holding back a
yard or so from the brink, nervous like her mother used
to get in the days when they used to go on family holidays and her father used to park the car overlooking a
steep headland. "Don't get too close, Frank, or else we
might go over."

A surface of water some twelve feet in diameter, impossible even to guess its depth. "Your father's not here,
Elsie." And then she noticed something floating, half
submerged in the water.

*She stared, wished that she hadn't, wished she had re-
fused to come anywhere near this dreadful place. An arm
casually flung out, a twisted leg protruding . . . a head,
the orifices black cavities as though fierce deepwater pike*

*had fed and bloated themselves. A hairless skull, the flesh
greenish with decomposition or gangrene.*

A body! Thelma Brown screamed, lurched and almost
fell, was going to be sick at any second, would probably
have thrown up except that her stomach was empty.

"There's somebody down there," she said turning to
the child who was now at her side. "Somebody who has
been dead for a long time."

"I told you my daddy was down there but you
wouldn't believe me." A mild reprimand. "I kept on telling you my daddy was in the garden." Not a hint of grief
or revulsion, more than an acceptance of a gruesome fact,
almost a gleeful statement. "Now do you want to see my
mummy's grave?"

"No!" Thelma swayed, closed her eyes. "I do not want
to see anybody's grave. That man in there, if it *is* a man,
has been dead for a very long time. We shall have to
report it to the police." And for Christ's sake where *are*
the police?

"It's my daddy." Stubborn, sullen.

"No, it's not, don't be silly."

"It *is!*" Elsie shouted, stamped her feet.

"All right, it's your daddy." Thelma closed her eyes
momentarily. "How did he come to fall in there?"

"I pushed him in!"

Thelma's heart stalled, charged up into a faster gear.
No, it couldn't be. This girl was mentally subnormal. She
had found the corpse, invented this story and was determined to live it out. It wasn't healthy. She's likely to fly
into a tantrum so I'd better continue to humor her.

"All right, you pushed him in, but what on earth for?"

*"Because he killed my mummy. Her grave's just over
there."*

God Almighty, this was getting crazier by the second!

I've looked at your father but the last thing I want to see is . . .

"Look, *there!*"

Thelma turned her head, saw the fresh mound of soil only ten yards away. She swallowed, tried to will it to disappear, just to be a heap of soil. But it didn't and it *was* a grave. A crude wooden crucifix at the one end, a macabre wreath weaved out of rushes.

"I'm making another wreath," Elsie said. "That one isn't much good, I did it in too much of a hurry because I wanted to put something on the grave. My daddy didn't like it. He was going to kill me too."

"How awful!"

"He had another woman. He was going to run away with her but first he had to get rid of mummy. So he brought her for a walk in here to help him get some firewood and then he hit her with the ax, chopped her up into tiny pieces. But at least he buried her."

Thelma heaved. It wasn't true, it couldn't be. The girl ought to be taken home to her parents (they were still alive somewhere), or else taken into care.

"Then he said that mummy was in the wood, wanted to talk to me so I went with him. He had the ax, was going to chop me up, too, but I pushed him down there. Look, there's the ax still lying on the ground."

A morbid compulsion had Thelma looking where the other pointed, tensing as she saw the ax lying in the grass. A stail that had almost rotted off, a brownish-red rusty head. It was rust, it *was.* Elsie had a vivid imagination, backed it up with any exhibit she could find; the body of an unknown man, she might even have dug that mound herself to support her story, and she'd found an ax which had lain forgotten since the last of the Droys worked this woodland. A fabrication, a good one, but a fantasy never-theless.

"How long ago did all this happen?" Play along with her. In all probability she knew the way out of here. She just needed coaxing.

"A few days ago, maybe a week."

"But that man down there's been dead for weeks, maybe months!" Oh Jesus, I've put my foot in it again, contradicted her.

"It was last week!" A shout, the beginning of another tantrum. "Maybe not even as long as that."

"Where did your daddy work?" Try and steer her off this macabre subject gently.

"Here, in this wood. He was the Droy Estate wood-man."

But the Droys haven't worked the wood since the turn of the century, maybe even earlier than that! Lies, every-thing she says is a lie.

"I see. Do you know the way out of the wood, Elsie?" Thelma held her breath, the million-dollar question. Or are you just hopelessly lost like me?

"There is no way out when the mist covers the wood!" She might have been reciting from the blackboard in the classroom, words that you learned, remembered and re-peated again and again.

There is no way out when the mist covers the wood!

"Who brought you here then, Elsie?"

"My daddy, I told you, so that he could chop me up and bury me like he buried mummy."

She's not just ninepence for a shilling, she's stark rav-ing mad!

"Well, we'll have to try and find a way out."

"There isn't one, don't you listen to what I tell you. Are you some kind of idiot?"

"But you came here?"

"With my daddy, are you stupid?" Shrieking now, that tiny face screwed up into a mask of anger.

"So you've been here ever since you . . . pushed your daddy in there?"

"You've got it"—a glance heavenward—"at last."

Thelma was trying to think. If only she knew in which direction the road lay she could grab Elsie by the hand, drag her forcibly along with her. But she didn't know. They might walk seaward, be even more hopelessly lost when night fell. Oh God, what were the police doing? They should have been scouring these woods by now, tracker dogs barking. Fillery didn't seem the sort just to give up.

"And I think I know who *you* are." Elsie's eyes slitted, her young lips curling into a sneer. "Oh yes, you couldn't be anybody else. I should have realized when I first saw you."

"Oh, and who do you think I am then?" Mild humor, awaiting a spate of further wild stories, more petulance.

"You're the woman my daddy was going to run off with, the reason he murdered mummy and tried to kill me. Aren't you? And don't lie. He used to sneak off from his work and meet you in the wood, didn't he? *That's the truth, isn't it?"*

"You're just being silly," she said, trying to laugh it off. "I never even knew your daddy, let alone met him secretly in the wood."

"You are!" She spat. "I know because you wouldn't be walking around naked like that if you weren't. Once my daddy was a good man, mummy said so, until *you,"*—stabbing an accusing finger, punching the air—"until *you* seduced him, poisoned his mind. You made him kill mummy!"

"That's ridiculous." Thelma found herself backing away.

"Witch!"

Suddenly Elsie had become a frightening prospect, much more than just a spoiled child getting into tantrums over her fantasies. Her face had aged, her expression blazed the malevolence of maturity. And with that came the realization that she was dangerous.

"The police will be here soon. They're already looking for me," Thelma Brown blurted out, stepped back another pace.

"The police!" This time the young girl's spittle hit her, an act of defiance and contempt. "The police won't come, and even if they do they won't find us. *Everybody is lost when the mist enshrouds Droy Wood!"*

Thelma found herself staring into those eyes which no longer belonged to a child. Pupils that dilated and contracted alternately so that you couldn't stop watching them, seemed to come out at you, bore into you; spun your brain so that you were nodding, speaking, saying things that you would not otherwise have said.

"Yes, I'm the woman you mentioned." Guilt, you couldn't hold back a lie. "I used to meet your daddy in the wood. I wanted to run away with him because I was having his baby. I wanted him for my own but first we had to kill your mother. We'd have killed you, too, only you were too smart for us."

"I was too smart for you." A peal of hysterical piping laughter. "I'm condemned to live in Droy Wood forever but *so are you!* None of us will ever leave but you will suffer torments worse than mine. Now, go and join your illicit lover in the pit, lie with him in the filth of your own making. Scream, but nobody will come. He screams for mercy every night but nobody hears him. *Go join him!"*

Thelma was aware that her legs were moving, propelled by a force beyond her own control. She tried to brace herself but she was powerless to halt the pushing, driving power that emanated from those crazed infantile eyes. Backward. And still backward!

"No, please!" She thought she screamed but it may have been in her own mind, an intention that got no further than a thought. Another step. And another.

She swayed, knew she was tottering on the brink, a wave of vertigo hitting her, pushing her. A scream but it was in the mind again. She felt herself go, head-first; and in that instant the spell was broken but it was too late.

A flash of memory, that time when one of her schoolgirl friends had pushed her in the deep end at the swimming baths. Her scream cut short by a mouthful of water, swallowing the chlorine-tasting liquid, panicking in a green underwater world, sinking until she bumped gently on the bottom. Then hands had grabbed her, pulled her up to the surface, helped her onto the side.

But this time there would be no rescuer. The black water seemed to leap up to meet her. How deep, oh Jesus, how deep? I can't swim!

She hit the water hard, felt the impact and then something soft was cushioning her fall. Mud, thick black mud, shooting everywhere, sucking noisily for her, gurgling. Floundering but sinking no further, two feet of water at the most, spitting out the vile-tasting fluid. Breathless, frightened, looking about her. Seeing . . .

She screamed properly this time. That partly decomposed corpse had reared up on a wave caused by her fall, a grotesque thing whose limp arms lifted and fell, the head jerking back and forth like a string puppet, water trickling from the open mouth. Watching her. No, it

couldn't see. It could. Toppling, floating again in a macabre crawl stroke, *coming toward her.*

*I want to touch you, to hold you, to mate with you, my
dearest. We have been apart too long. This is our joyous
reunion brought about by my evil daughter and the two of
us shall be together for all time.*

Fingers touched her thigh but somehow she squirmed
away, managed to stand upright. Her left ankle shot
pains up her leg, she must have twisted it in the fall.
Trying to run, hobbling, splashing, forcibly dragging her
feet out of the mud. One way, then another, trapped in a
prison whose walls were solid mud with a demented creature that had risen from its watery grave.

Tiring, but her pursuer seemed tireless, bubbling black
water out of the cavities that had once been nostrils and
mouth, following her every movement with those empty
eye sockets. Eager, lusting, wearing her down.

And up above the child who had called herself Elsie
leaned over and watched, laughing insanely with obvious
glee.

"The two of you are together at last," she screeched,
her shrill piping tones seeming to whistle in the deep pit-
hole. "That was what you wanted, wasn't it? But you
won't have a second to yourselves because I'm going to
be right here watching you. I'm going to see all those
things you used to do together when you sneaked off into
the wood. You'll be together for always but I'll be right
here. You can't escape from the pit but even if you did
you'll never leave the wood. Because nobody leaves Droy
Wood—*ever!*"

Shrill peals of mirth that vibrated in Thelma Brown's
brain, hurt her. Splashing, running still but slowing

down. Her ankle was swelling up fast so that she could barely rest her weight on it.

And then those gnarled icy hands grabbed her, pulled her back, twisted her round. Helplessly she watched those slobbering lips coming in search of her own.

TEN

Detective-Constable Alan Lee sat on the cold muddy bank of a reedy bog and buried his face in his hands. The girl was gone, lost forever perhaps just as the others were. And it was all his fault; he let himself go, wept. Sobbing, contemplating suicide, wondering if he had the courage. He did not think so.

He had seen the plane crash, watched in bewilderment as the parachutist had come sailing down. And after that he knew that he had to be crazy. They would have to lock him away somewhere where he couldn't do anybody any harm.

He tried to think logically, piece together the events of the past few hours. Jesus, to think he'd done *that* to the girl! It was unbelievable. *You are charged with rape and attempted murder!* No, it wasn't me, it was somebody else. It was you, Alan Lee, a police officer on duty who betrayed both the force and the public you serve. I tell you, I'm not guilty. *You have been found guilty and sentenced to . . .*

Sweating profusely. No such thing had been in his mind when he'd picked Thelma Brown out in the headlights, or even when she had got into the car. Not until *. . . he hit that bank of fog lying across the road!*

The transformation had been as sudden as that. Up until that moment his thoughts had been concentrated on the case in hand, negative ones. Reconstructions were a dicey business but there was always a slim chance. You only needed to jog one person's memory, the right person. In the States they sometimes used hypnosis on witnesses. Whatever the method all you needed was one clue that would lead you to the killer. But it had been a foul night when Carol Embleton had disappeared and in a village like Droy most people would have gone to bed. But now the police were trying a long shot; no real harm if it didn't come off. Nothing to lose.

Those clothes of Foster's gave him an uncomfortable feeling, made him think about the man himself. A pervert, a mind that would defy all the efforts of psychiatrists, he had to be locked away and kept there for the rest of his life. A judge had been lenient and now they had a murder on their hands and two missing people as well. It could be, and probably was, a triple murder case now.

The moment he drove into that bank of mist Alan Lee began to understand Foster, not consciously but picking up wavelengths. It began with an erection, followed by a sideways glance at the girl by his side. God, she was beautiful; he envisioned her naked, lying beneath him, responding, urging him on. He came pretty close to an ejaculation just thinking about it.

The car was stationary, just the facia lights left on giving a dim glow. They could be here a long time, just the two of them. Maybe she fancied him too. And if she didn't . . .

Just touching her was electrifying him and he knew that kiss he forced upon her wasn't going to be enough. Then she'd started playing the hard-to-get game. She wanted him really, of course she did. A bit of playing about is fine but if it goes on too long it gets very frustrating. I want to screw you, baby, *please!* Well I'm going to whether you like it or not. Lust taking over. I don't want to think about the rest. Maybe it didn't happen, it was all a dream, a fantasy. But it did, that's why you're here now shivering in the nude, lost in a wooded marsh, and she's out there somewhere. Foster, too; he might already have killed her.

And that plane crash. It had all gone quiet now, not a sound to be heard except the steady dripping of condensation off the trees. There should have been sirens wailing, crowds gathering. It couldn't have been more than half a mile away. But there was nothing except the stillness of a foggy night.

He had to find the girl. Maybe if he could just talk to her, try to explain. Look, I'm sorry, I didn't mean to rape you. Can't we settle this business without reporting it? I've got a bit of cash saved up and I'm prepared to be generous. I'm not like you think I am, really. But she wouldn't understand. All the same he had to find her because for the moment he was still a policeman.

It was making a valiant attempt to get light, a weak grayness in which you could just make out silhouettes, trees and tall reeds. It doesn't matter much which way you go, but you'll have to tread quietly. If she hears you she'll hide; you're the last person on earth she wants to meet right now.

Moving slowly, his bare feet sinking in the mud, making glugging noises as he extricated them. This was a path of some kind, God knows who made it. Follow it all the same.

Drier ground, probably higher than the rest, piles of leaves that rustled. It was getting much lighter now.

A cry, so faint at first that it might have been the calling of some distant sea bird. Echoing in his brain. He stood still, head cocked to one side, listening. The roaring in his ears didn't help. It was probably his imagination—

like the plane crash and that bloke parachuting down out of the sky. This place did strange things to you, there was no doubt about that.

He heard it again, louder this time and he knew instantly that it was real. A scream. Christ, Thelma Brown was in some kind of desperate trouble. A flash of hope for himself; it had to be Foster and nailing that bastard could solve a lot of problems. A scapegoat if Thelma was already dead, leniency if she wasn't and he saved her. *Look, kid, I'm not like that really. Suppose we just forget about what happened last night.*

He broke into a run, ducking beneath low branches, suddenly the trained policeman again. Remembering that he had been armed at the start of this mission; his pistol was still in the car. He had nothing except himself, not even his clothes. Foster was nude, too, unless he had found some garments in the meantime. A confrontation that might have been taking place thousands of years ago, man against man in a primitive land.

She was screaming hysterically now, the mist muffling her yells to some extent. Not far away now, a hundred yards at the most.

Seconds later he burst into the wide clearing, his sweeping gaze taking in everything. A deep hole of some kind, that was where the screams were coming from; she was still screaming. Swirling mist as though that pit boiled and was giving off clouds of vile-smelling steam. A half-light; was it really light, did it ever get any different in this place, or had it been light for hours and this was how it always was, a depressing timelessness?

Alan Lee was moving toward the pit when he noticed the man standing on the opposite side watching him, recognizing him instantly. *It was James Foster!*

The other was naked, wild in appearance as though he

had lived this way for months, his body caked with dried mud. There was a mark on his throat; it looked like a wide gash that had bled and congealed. A scratch perhaps, inflicted by a trailing briar; it couldn't have been very deep, the policeman reflected, otherwise he would have bled to death in a matter of minutes.

Lee's keen trained eye noted something else, brought a grimace to his lips as well as a sense of guilt. The rapist had a full erection. *Just like I did last night.*

The girl was down there somewhere. What the hell was going on?

"You're just in time, copper," a taunting maniacal laugh from Foster. "She's down there now and he's raping her!"

Lee froze with indecision. Across the gulf stood the man who was currently Public Enemy Number One. Within his grasp. Down below Thelma Brown was being raped by . . . someone. Go for Foster and you could be too late. Save the girl and you'll probably lose him. A dilemma requiring a split-second decision. Save the girl!

Detective-Constable Alan Lee ran for the side, stared down into the depths of that murky pit-hole, recoiled at what he saw. It had to be another nightmare for no way could anything exist like *that!* Human in shape, a grotesque figure that dripped slime, covered in black mud, bearing the screaming girl down into the shallow water, her struggles threshing it to a foam, sending up foul odors. Fighting to keep her head out of the water, perhaps her mind had already snapped.

"You see it?" Foster called jubilantly. "He's raping her, copper. And I'll bet right now if she had the chance she'd change him for me. Or *you!*" Peals of insane laughter. "What's it feel like to be a rapist, copper? They'll give you fifteen years, maybe life if that girl dies, because *you* killed her. *Just remember that, you're a murderer, just like me!"*

But Alan Lee wasn't listening. He was fighting to drag his brain back into action, break the spell of petrification, dismissing Foster; he had to save Thelma Brown. His eyes flicked round the top of the pit once, a vain hope that there might be a ladder or even a rope handy. There wasn't and he knew then what he had to do.

That creature had her head under the muddy water now, deliberately drowning her while he lifted the lower half of her body up, a kind of wheelbarrow stance that facilitated the backward and forward movements of his filthy thighs. Slamming faster and faster, rotted lungs wheezing loudly under the strain. Oh you filthy fucking bastard, you've no right to exist! Maybe you don't and it's another trick of this bloody fog, but whether it is or not the girl is going to die if I don't do something fast.

Lee balanced himself, took a deep breath. Don't think about it or else you'll chicken out. You're demonstrating a life-saving exercise to a bunch of rookies at the baths. You're on the high springboard. Nothing to it, just don't look down. Fill your lungs, relax your muscles as you go; go right down and come up fast.

Airborne, somersaulting once, judging the distance in his own mind. Lukewarm chlorinated water that'll make your eyes smart. *Impact!*

A soft landing that threw him flat, reality coming back as he wallowed in the mud, clawed himself up to the surface. It sucked viciously and he knew he had gone in above his knees, was temporarily trapped in the morass. Take it easy, struggle too hard and you'll sink deeper. Move the right leg a few inches, now the left, work your way steadily upward. Then lie flat and ease yourself out;

training instructions for rescuing people trapped in quicksands, as per manual.

The thing in the pit was aware of his presence, turned slowly, released the girl and she flopped back down into the water, lay partly submerged, face downward. Not moving, half-floating. *Oh Jesus, I'm too late, she's already dead!*

Stupefaction bordering on hypnosis as Detective-Constable Alan Lee stared up into the malevolent features of a behemoth in human form. A vile stinking body, from the pelvis downward just skeletal; that inhuman sex act had been a pointless simulation then, a last blasphemous attempt at procreation. Symbolic rape.

Bubbles formed and burst on nose and mouth cavities, eye sockets pouring watery filth like acute conjunctivitis, that wheezing now a liquid sound. Advancing unsteadily, arms stretched out toward the man helplessly trapped in the mud.

The policeman knew that his brain had to snap, that it had reached the limit of human endurance, could not accept what it saw. Lying forward, the way the manual taught you, but his legs still wouldn't come free. Laughter somewhere reminding him of the taped mirth producers use to boost unfunny comedy films on TV. Laugh or we'll laugh for you. Foster, of course, up there savoring every second. Just remember you're a murderer, copper. She's dead and *you* killed her.

Lee closed his eyes for a second, one last try, and then he opened them again. "I'm a police officer."

The other took another step, coughed up a solid lump of slime that plopped into the water.

"D'you hear me, I'm a police officer! You're under arrest, for rape and murder." Stop that fucking laughing up

there, I'm serious. *"Anything you say will be taken down and may be used in evidence against you."*

It towered over him now, Christ it had to be well over six feet tall, a colossus that pissed stagnant water all over you. Cold stinking water, the stench making you retch. Lee pulled for all he was worth, got his right leg almost free; the mud beneath him shifted, started to suck it back down again.

A noise to his left; Thelma had submerged, rolled over, surfaced again, was floating free on her back, arms stretched right out over her head as though she were doing the backstroke, staring vacantly up at the lowering gray sky above the pit. A rush of trapped air made bubbles on the water, big ones that burst slowly one at a time. She might not be dead yet, very close but not quite. I've got to give her artificial respiration, it's my duty. Get out of the way, you bugger, let me go to her.

"You're bloody well under arrest!"

Crying hysterically now, not caring for himself when a huge hand reached out, caught him by the hair and jerked his head back, almost dislocating his vertebrae. Hair came out by the roots, floated on the surface like the feathers of a mallard in molt. Still telling the fucker he was under arrest, that he had to accompany him to the station where he would be required to make a statement. Some bugger was still laughing, jeering. Their mates always acted up when you arrested one of them. Ignore it, get on with your job.

Fingers prised his mouth open; he tried to bite on them but it didn't seem to make any difference. A sudden snap, instant pain and his jaw wasn't working anymore, a ventriloquist's dummy that had bust a spring. But the show went on.

The creature was bending down, scooping up handfuls

of cold black mud, feeding them into that open limp mouth, stuffing the morass in with its fingers, shoving it right down the back of its victim's throat. Handful after handful, poking it up the nostrils, a macabre nose-pick in reverse.

The policeman was not struggling any longer, gasping one last time for breath and then giving up, accepting that he was going to suffocate. With bulging eyes that threatened to pop at any second he studied the limp floating figure of the girl. She had touched the far wall of the pit and it had swung her round; she was coming back this way. Almost doing the splits, letting him feast his eyes on her ravaged flesh, a final act of revenge even after death.

Take a good look, Constable. I'm all torn about, still bleeding. *You* did that to me. Not him, because he doesn't have anything left to do it with. You tricked me, took advantage of your position and the situation. Now I'm dead and you're not far off. I'll give you another thirty seconds at the most. Neither of us will be leaving here. We'll be down here forever with *that,* and eventually we'll become like him. Just waiting for somebody else to fall in here and then we'll fight like hell over them. Bye for now, copper, you dirty bastard. See you soon.

Alan Lee tried to scream one last yell of remorse, wanted her to understand how it had all come about, but the effort was too much for him. And even after the constable died, foul mud was still being crammed into his mouth, slipping steadily down his throat and into his lungs.

Up above, the man who had once been James Foster turned away and walked off into the dense fog, idly fingering at the open bloodless wound in his throat, a subconscious action which was fast becoming a habit with him.

ELEVEN

Andy Dark eyed the German with both fear and amazement, watched the steady, gloating descent down the stairs. The conservation officer glanced once behind him toward the open door. If it had not been for that menacing Luger in the other's hand he would have grabbed Carol and taken pot luck on a dash for freedom. But for her sake he dared not chance it.

"So, my prison cannot hold you." Bertie Hass reached the bottom step, advancing slowly on them. "You British are all the same, you will never accept the inevitable. Even now in the face of defeat you fight on, risk annihilation. A mad race of people."

"You're crazy," Andy snapped, pulling Carol behind him. "The war's been over nearly forty years. Germany was beaten. Your beloved Führer made one big mistake, he chose to go for Russia before Britain and underestimated the winter. Just like Napoleon did."

"Silence!" For a second that forefinger threatened to tighten on the trigger. "How dare you speak of the Führer with such lies. No decision has yet been made concerning an assault on Stalin . . . at least, if it has, then the details have not been released." A flicker of uncertainty in those pale blue eyes but it went as quickly as it came.

"All right, have it your own way." Andy sighed, shrugging his shoulders with a casualness which he certainly did not feel. "Britain is facing defeat, you've caught us escaping from your own private POW camp, so what now?"

"You are spies." The Luftwaffe pilot's gaze flicked over the cowering girl. "And most fortunately for myself the Gestapo will be arriving here shortly. They are experts at dealing with your kind, breaking your stubborn spirit. In the meantime let us go into the room behind you, it will be more comfortable than standing out here in the hall."

The room leading off the hall was some kind of library, Andy Dark noted with surprise, oak-paneled walls that had the appearance of having been recently polished, floor-to-ceiling shelves lined with leather-bound, gold-tooled books. You saw the spines, had a feeling that that was all they were; a façade, a pseudo-accumulation of literary works that a stagehand might stack in a dusty storeroom after the last performance. A wide latticed window behind the roll-top desk. And a musty smell as though this place had been shut up for years.

"Listen," Bertie Hass held up a hand, "can you not hear it?"

Carol Embleton thought at first that thunder was rumbling somewhere, a distant electric storm beyond Droy Wood. Oh God, anybody who was away from the wood did not realize how lucky they were. It was dark outside except for flashes lighting up the sky, becoming more frequent by the second. *That was crazy, it couldn't be dark yet, back in the hall dim gray light had been filtering in!*

The noises outside were familiar, hit her with a force that had her clinging to Andy, whispering: "It's the bombing again and any second . . ."

They were all staring out of the window at the fiery sky, watching, waiting. Carol knew what they would see, any second now. A feeling you got when you lit a firework that you knew was going to go off with a loud explosion, bracing yourself for the ear-bursting bang.

"There it is," she breathed, "the bomber. Any second it's going to burst into flames, crash. And . . . *he* will parachute down!"

They heard the approaching plane and then they saw it, an inferno, disintegrating, showering earthward until it was lost from view behind the dark outline of the wood, the sky now a blaze of different shades of orange and yellow. A tiny floating figure, his fall so gradual and graceful. There was no doubt that he would drop in Droy Wood.

Carol glanced behind her, her skin prickling when she saw the German still standing there. *You're not supposed to be here, you should be out there. How can you be in two places at the same time?*

"And still the British resist." Bertie Hass laughed scornfully. "See, a lucky shot has claimed one of the Luftwaffe bombers, another crew has died valiantly for the Fatherland. Their Iron Crosses will be awarded post-humously."

"But . . . but what about the survivor?" Carol breathed. "Are you going to try and find him?"

"What survivor?"

A defiant hiss, almost petulant. Childish. *No, I don't see anything, daddy, and nothing you can say will make me see it.* "There were no survivors, an entire crew killed in glorious action."

"But . . . one of them parachuted down." *You,* but even I can't accept that.

"Nobody parachuted from that plane. If you saw any-thing then it was an illusion."

"We must have imagined it," Andy Dark cut in. He didn't like the way the barrel of the Luger had swung back on to them. Provocation could mean instant death. "I guess you're right, nobody got out of that plane. They're all dead by now."

But Bertie Hass was clearly shaken. There was no doubt that he had seen that lone figure drifting down out of the sky. He licked his lips nervously, moved back to the window and stared out, his face briefly against the glass but it did not mist up. Searching the blackness for . . . *himself?*

Andy Dark tensed, reckoned he could have jumped the other, almost acted impetuously. If Carol had not been here he probably would have risked it. That wasn't the only reason that stopped him, though. Watching Hass, seeing how the other's features changed, almost as though he did not want to look, was afraid to. Flinching, cowering, beginning to tremble as he followed the course the silhouetted bomber pilot had taken against the fiery sky. Eyes glazing . . .

Bertie Hass felt the rush of cold air, braced himself again for the bone-shattering impact as he struck the ground, hoped that he would be killed instantly, not left a mangled heap of bloody flesh and bones with life refusing to desert him.

A welcome jerk snatching him up, knocking the breath from his body, knowing that he wasn't going to die after all. Exhilaration, a feeling of freedom which only the free-faller and the birds of the air know. Only briefly, though, because already the topmost branches of the wood were clawing for him, trying to claim him for their own; grotesque shapes that were more than just trees.

Down; struggling in the mud, extricating himself from the bog, slashing at his parachute cords to free himself. The mist was thickening, he had come to accept it now. Everything so familiar, an actor on stage for a nightly performance of a long-running play. Almost boring, wishing that you had the courage to change your lines just to alleviate it. But you couldn't.

That feeling of being watched again, finding the muddy path and following it, knowing that it would bring him out at the big house, a ruin that would be transformed. His home until the war ended. It would be over soon, the British could not hold out much longer, they were on their knees already.

Listening. He could not hear the bombing anymore. Glancing up, the sky was dark, overcast. The city still burned though; he could smell the acrid stench in his nostrils, coughed. Frustration, an urgency to forge on ahead, begin the setting up of his new headquarters in preparation for the coming of the German army but knowing that he had to wait. Because the girl would be coming, naked and beautiful, reminding him of Ingrid, having to fight against a stirring of his emotions because the Fatherland was a priority. The girl would be locked away, a pleasure to be savored later.

The actor rushing his lines, harassing the other performers because he wanted to get this early act over and done with. A blurred film like a screaming express train on the screen, only slowing down at the whim of the projectionist. Pulse racing, finally sighing with relief, sweating.

The girl was a prisoner in the dungeon. Bertie Hass had resisted the temptation to run his fingers over her bare flesh as she hung there on the wall. There would be ample time to indulge in those pleasures later. The trap door thudded shut, echoed eerily down the empty hallway. He shivered, the sound had a note of finality about it. He knew only too well what was going to happen next, the principal actor regretting his haste; he didn't really like this part of the play at all, wished somehow the producers could have skipped it, altered the script. He knew that at any second that oaken door on his left was going to creak open . . . No, not this time. *Mein Gott,* no! He slid the Luger out of his holster, trained the barrel on the doorway, a marksman's stance, gripping his right wrist with the fingers of his left hand.

The oak door started to open, easing inward, groaning as if those hinges had not swung back for centuries. The German's finger tightened on the trigger. *This time do not delay, fire the moment you see it or it will be too late once again!*

A bulky figure filled the widening gap. A florid bad-tempered face with a series of jowls unfolding below the chin, eyes almost buried in the fleshy cheeks yet penetrating, commanding; angry. Strange silken garments, gold buttons straining on a scarlet waistcoat, cream breeches that were laced below the knee, silk stockings, and hide slippers.

Fire now or your chance is gone!

The German's trigger finger was stiff as though it had suddenly become afflicted with arthritis. He had to force the joints to move, use every vestige of willpower he could muster, wilting beneath the force of those piglike eyes. The Luger crashed, bucked, crashed again. Heavy slugs ripped into the woodwork of the door, threw it back, the man still standing there as though totally unaware of what was happening.

At this range Bertie Hass knew he could not miss. The trigger was becoming tighter with each shot, any second it would seize up. Now his shots were finding their mark, tearing into those fine clothes, shredding them, lacerating the fleshy jowls; three head shots but the stranger was still on his feet, not even swaying. He had to be dead, it was only his nerves that were holding him upright. He had to fall any second. A shot disintegrated the top of his head and he appeared to totter, grabbed at a doorpost to steady himself.

"Die!" Bertie yelled, and then the firing pin was clicking harmlessly. Disbelief, watching, waiting but still those eyes focused on him, angrily, mocking him. You can't kill me, German!

You're dead, you've got to be. Then came an awful realization that had the pistol dropping from the pilot's nerveless fingers, clanging on the floor. Those terrible wounds . . . *they did not bleed!*

How long he stood there he had no idea. Daylight faded into darkness and became light again. And now the man in the doorway had moved out into the hallway and that was when Bertie Hass would have run screaming from this place, only his limbs refused to move. *Those terrible wounds had knitted, healed, not so much as a scar showing.*

"You can't kill me, German." The stranger's tones were thick and nasal, thin lips twisted into a cruel smile. "Nobody can die when they are already dead, can they?"

The Luftwaffe man's brain did not seem to be functioning, accepting the situation rather than trying to understand it. Nodding. Of course it was impossible to die if you were already dead.

"We were expecting you," he said. The big man's waistcoat strained. "But I don't expect you even know who I am."

"No, sir." Embarrassed, humble like that time the Führer had let his eyes rest upon him during the course of a Luftwaffe parade. Like God himself; you would have died there and then, unquestioningly, if he had asked you.

"I am Ross Droy, the owner of these lands on which you have trespassed." A throaty laugh. "The last stronghold of the Droys, a bastion which will never fall. Our lands have been stolen, sold off by those who had no right to the title, but they will never take the wood from us. Not even your German army if they conquer Britain."

Bertie flinched slightly but did not reply.

"Our war has raged for centuries," and the other waved a hand nonchalantly, "but still we survive. We can use you, stranger, indeed we shall use you. Look upon this place as your own, deal harshly with any who infiltrate it. There are others who live here, too, from time to time. My officers are vigilant against those who would use our lands for bringing in contraband from other countries, but unfortunately . . . they are not always available," another wave of that podgy hand, "they . . . come and go. But the lands of my ancestors must be protected at all times. Remember that when the mist rolls in from the marshes . . ."

And suddenly Ross Droy wasn't there anymore. Bertie Hass had not seen him go. The door was still open, affording him a view of the interior, a richly furnished book-lined study with a wide latticed window overlooking the wood. Possibly one could see the marsh from here on clear days. An empty room. Nobody here, even the bullet gouges on the woodwork had disappeared. It might have been a hallucination; the German tried to convince himself that that was what it was. The war took its toll of battle-scarred veterans in a number of inexplicable ways.

Except that this was no illusion. Over the weeks, months, years, he had seen the other guardians of the Droy lands, ones who walked the mist, inflicted terrible atrocities upon those who fell into their clutches. And the Customs men who dragged their screaming victims down into the dungeons, left them there to rot. You heard their pathetic cries, smelled the rotting corpses but when you went to look there was nothing there except dust and decay. Prisoners never left the dungeons. Until now. Somehow the girl and this young man had survived.

It worried Bertie Hass, something was changing here. You could sense it. And now tonight he had witnessed his own leap from the blazing bomber, seen himself parachuting down into the wood. He didn't know what it all meant, was frightened to think about it. Perhaps these two strangers could help him.

"Nobody has ever escaped from Droy Wood." Bertie Hass's voice had dropped to a whisper, an echo of the hopelessness which had lurked deep inside him ever since he had dropped in here out of the night sky, discovered this place of eternal mists with its unknown terrors. Those terrors had dominated him; he had just refused to acknowledge them, an indoctrinated Nazi who lived in the hope of his freedom when the German army arrived. But it had been a long time coming. He had to face up to the fact, a lingering doubt which he had refused to admit even to himself, that the Nazis wouldn't be coming.

"I reckon we could make it." Andy Dark tried to speak casually. "You, Carol and me. If we stuck together we'd have a better chance. We've got to do something, we can't just stop here. Time's running out . . . even for you."

"Tell me." There was reluctance in the German's tone. "What . . . what happened . . . how did the war end?"

"Germany was beaten," Andy responded, trying to refrain from gloating. "As I told you the Führer's big mistake was . . ."

"The Führer does not make mistakes!" The pistol came up again.

"Perhaps he was ill-advised." Andy held Carol close to him; Christ, we can't go into all that again. "The German army floundered in the snows of a Russian winter and the Allied forces won the war in Europe. Then the Americans dropped two atom bombs on Japan. After that the result of the war was a foregone conclusion."

Bertie Hass's features whitened, his mouth puckered, and for a moment the other two thought that he was going to burst into tears. The Luger dangled, he almost dropped it. Sadness, his dreams crashing, his ambitions shattered. "And the Luftwaffe?"

"They don't exist anymore. Germany was split into two, east and west, a diabolical wall built through Berlin to segregate them. Britain is at peace with West Germany but the eastern half is now a part of the Soviet bloc. Russia is now the main threat to world peace."

"*If* what you say is true," and you could just be lying, "then I have no Fatherland to return to." There was a pleading in his expression which almost had Carol Embleton feeling sorry for him. She tried to forget those awful hours spent in the blackness of a stinking, rat-infested dungeon.

"I am sure your country will welcome you back and honor the service you gave." For once in my life I've got to toady to somebody, Andy thought. He's actually believed us, accepted the truth.

"Then we must try to leave Droy Wood." Hass glanced back toward the window. Outside it was dark again, no sign of distant fires, no sound of whining spitfires, droning bombers. No explosions. "We must go now before it is too late." He tensed, was the Luftwaffe pilot of World War II again, the pistol jerking back up to cover them.

"But I warn you, if this is some contrived ruse to make me assist you in escaping from a place which I believed was German occupied territory then you will die instantly. I promise you that I shall not await the arrival of the Gestapo."

"Fair enough," Andy nodded, "but we'd better move fast. We've talked too long already."

Bertie Hass motioned with his gun for them to walk in front of him, a trio in single file crossing the large room. Since they had been in here it seemed to have aged, deteriorated; the paneling no longer glistened with fresh polish, it was stained and dirty, eroded with the efforts of woodworm. And everywhere smelled stale and musty. They moved out into the hall.

Andy strained at the heavy door, thought for one awful moment that it was barred but then it swung back, protesting loudly, the hinges squeaking as though they had not moved for decades. A rush of cold air hit them, damp with the foul marsh mist that still enshrouded the wood. In any other situation he would have suggested that they awaited the dawn but there was no time. You had a strange feeling that something was about to happen, that the evil in this place was building up to a terrible climax.

"Which way?" he muttered.

The German hesitated, scanned the sky, searching for just one glimmer, one reflection from a burning city; listening for the dull thumping of distant exploding bombs. But there was nothing; nothing to give them a clue to the direction they must take.

He moved ahead of the other two, somehow found the muddy track, the one that snaked away from Droy House and on through the reed-beds. It could have led anywhere but they could not stay here.

A tramping and squelching of feet, hurrying even though they did not know where they were going. They could feel and smell the fog in the blackness of a night which gave you the impression that it might never end. You knew you were lost, you just walked on and on and tried to hope when everything seemed hopeless . . .

Suddenly the silence of a long-dead place was broken, a sound that seemed to be everywhere and yet nowhere in particular, even the thick fog unable to muffle it. *A howling that rose up like the foul-smelling marsh gases, came at them viciously, venomously, had Carol Embleton screaming. The noise reached its peak, began again, even louder, a chorus now.*

You heard it, you felt it, you wanted to flee blindly even though you knew you could not escape from it. It was in front of you, behind you, closing in on you, numbing your brain, freezing your limbs.

"What is it?" Carol screamed a second time. "Andy, whatever is it?"

"It sounds like . . ." Don't panic, it can't be, not here in England. And yet it had to be. When one has taken a degree in zoology, studied animals of the wild from the continents of the world, their habits and sounds, the answer is there before you—however much you try to reject it. You want to disbelieve but in the end you believe because there is no alternative. "It sounds like . . . *a pack of wolves!*"

He grabbed her hand, ran for the faint silhouette of a tall oak with low spreading branches, a tree that had overcome the growth stunting of its neighbors. A headlong dash through deep mud, knowing that he and Carol must climb to safety before they were torn apart.

Behind them they heard the report of the Luger as Bertie Hass began shooting.

TWELVE

Detective-Sergeant Jim Fillery had managed to snatch an hour's sleep in the chair in his temporary headquarters, a fitful slumber disturbed by the constant jangling of the telephone, people moving about, talking. He had learned to catnap, recharge his batteries in the minimum amount of time available to him, and his superiors begrudged him even that.

He stirred, saw that it was starting to get light. The pressure was really on him now, the media, everybody baying for his blood. You've lost five people and Foster is still at large. One wood, permanently cordoned off and you know they're in there. What the fuck are you playing at?

One more hunt, the biggest in recent history concentrated on such a small area. And if that didn't produce results . . . he didn't have any answer to that one. Today they would drag that wood out, uproot every tree and bush if they had to. But he still had that nagging feeling that they would not find anything. Your thinking's negative, he reprimanded himself. Think *positively!* We're bloody well going to find 'em, all of 'em, including Foster.

He poured himself a cup of black coffee, swigged it down. Calls were coming in all the time, the switchboard a nonstop panel of activity. Cranks, you always got 'em. I raped and killed the girl, *please* believe me, officer. I'll put it in writing and you can lock me away for the rest of my life; I don't mind so long as you believe what I say and give me the credit, tell the newspapers. There were a hundred confessions for every murder but you still had to sift through 'em until you found the one who denied the lot. You got hunches, followed 'em. Instinct. But right now Jim Fillery's instinct had dried up.

The whole of the county force, every man that could be spared and a lot who couldn't, had converged on Droy. The burglars and the car thieves would have a field day and good luck to them. The minute it was light enough they were going to rip that bloody wood wide open. A copper had gone missing and that counted for an awful lot where the boys were concerned, in some cases more than the two girls. Some bastard had got one of your colleagues, you might be the next . . . So you moved heaven and earth to find the killer.

Fillery couldn't work it out about PC Lee. One of the most promising young detectives in the force yet there was evidence that he had raped the decoy girl; they had both fled into the wood. We'll rip the fucking place right open, Fillery told himself. The way we're going to scour it today a vole couldn't escape undetected.

Damn this fog, wasn't it ever going to shift! Now its tentacles had stretched right up to the village, a vaporized monster extending its territory. These villagers were scared, most of 'em skulking in their cottages and flatly refusing to assist in any way.

"You won't get anybody from Droy to join in the hunt, Sarge." Eddie Farnett, the sub-postmaster, shook his head slowly, a half-burned cigarette perpetually bobbing in the center of his thick lips. "None of 'em will go within half a mile of the wood. It doesn't bother me, personally, but I can't get away from the post office. My wife doesn't like the post office work, she'll only look after the shop part, if you see what I mean. When we go on holiday or I'm ill, I have to get a temp in. But you can't get temps at a moment's notice, if you see what I mean. And you can't shut a post office up, can you?"

Excuses on tap, a ready-made cocoon. Jim Fillery saw what he meant all right, only too well. Just two locals among the large gathering on the road adjoining the wood. PC Houliston because he didn't have any choice; Roy Bean because secretly he resented this intrusion of his game preserves. He didn't go to Droy Wood in the course of his work but he objected to anybody else going there. They were trespassers whichever way you looked at it. Dogs in any woodland were a bloody nuisance except on shooting days; they ran about barking and disturbing every species of wildlife. In a way the wood was a useful reserve. Pheasants could breed safely in there during the summer months; the wood had its uses and today was going to undo all of them.

Muffin seemed strangely lethargic today, not even straining at the leash, keeping close to his heels as they split up in bunches for briefing. She didn't like the setup, that was only too clear. Cringing, tail between her legs. Silly bitch, but he felt uneasy, too. Like something was going to happen today, something awful.

A three-pronged "attack" was planned for today; Houliston had already left with fifty men, skirted the perimeter of the wood and gone out to the marsh. They would move inland, due north. Two lines of searchers, one from the east, the other from the west, everybody in due course converging in the center, approximately where the ruined house stood. Thirty dogs in all, a net which nobody could slip through, Fillery had told them and tried to sound confident. And after that they were going to drag every pool. Nobody mentioned the bogs because you couldn't do anything about *them.*

The mist was thicker than ever, had the density of an old-fashioned "pea-souper," a strange menacing purposefulness about the way it hung over the wood and the village, a deliberate obstruction to the hunters, hiding its terrible secrets. Elsewhere the atmosphere was dull and cloudy with normal visibility. That was what disturbed you most.

A long wait. Roy Bean tried to curb his own impatience. This was how the shooters felt when the beaters had to go out a long way in order to bring a patch of cover back toward them. Anticipation, then boredom. Today there was an added ingredient—fear!

At last they heard the whistle, a synchronization of all their respective lines, looking to the men on either side of them. Keep me in sight all the time, you guys. For Christ's sake don't leave me on my own. Always was scared of the dark and if this fog gets any thicker it'll be as good as night.

Moving forward, Alsatians, terriers unleashed and being encouraged to hunt for a scent. This time they just had to come up with something.

It had taken Jock Houliston over an hour to reach the outskirts of Droy Marsh following a circuitous route over the adjoining pastureland, always hoping he was going in the right direction because the fog gave you a feeling that your own personal radar wasn't working any longer. At last, though, they reached the narrow foreshore, stood with their backs to the sea, heard the tide but couldn't see it, an eerie watery wilderness lapping against the rocks. *It's trying to drive you back into the wood.* That's ridiculous because we're going there, anyway. Hurry then. Everybody looking about them but they could not see anything, not even the murky outline of Droy Wood.

A noise, one that you gradually became aware of, a splashing that wasn't just the waves on the shoreline. Rhythmic, forming a picture in your mind, a draw-by-dots kiddies' scene that had you penciling, joining up the dots eagerly, wondering what was going to unfold. A seascape . . . a *boat!* Houliston hesitated, half turned back. Of course, nobody had tumbled to it, not even those smart-aleck plainclothes detectives. It took an ordinary bobby in uniform to solve a case which had commanded the front pages of every daily newspaper for almost a week. *Foster had a boat, had lain low and now was making his escape by sea!*

The policeman's pulse raced and his hand went to his pocket radio. And stopped. No fear, not on your nellie! The bright boys would take all the credit with not a mention of your long-serving country copper. Well, this time they were going to end up with egg on their faces. PC Jock Houliston would make the arrest, he'd have the killer handcuffed before he . . . but he didn't have a boat and you couldn't chase anybody out to sea without one!

Swish . . . splash . . . swish . . . splash.

Louder! It should have grown fainter, as the boat gradually left the shore, barely discernible.

Swish . . . splash.

Houliston craned his neck, thought he could make out a shape in the fog; the boat, somebody hunched in it, heaving on a pair of heavy oars; *coming this way . . .*

Unbelievable but it was true. Whoever it was they were now scraping the bottom of their craft on the beach, jumping out, pulling it up out of the water. More than one of them . . . peering again. *Three* of them. Foster and . . . Five people had gone missing. Perm any three from five. Logically one of them had to be the rapist and that was all that mattered.

The policeman glanced behind him; there was no sign of the rest of the search party, the fog having swallowed them up. Not a sound except for that made by those with the boat. His hand caressed the flat oblong shape of his radio again. Not bloody likely, this was *his* show!

He crouched down, tried to make himself as inconspicuous as possible. They would come this way, all he had to do was to wait, loom out of the mist in front of them. His hand went into his pocket, jangled a pair of handcuffs faintly. Oh yes, the country copper would show them a thing or two.

Here they come now, two men and what looks like a boy. It might be one of the missing girls, a slip of a figure. No, Carol Embleton was a big girl, it couldn't be her. Thelma Brown then. Hell, it didn't matter just so long as one of them was James Foster, the most wanted man in Britain.

Their feet squelched in waterlogged grass, and they were muttering to one another. Furtive, stopping every few yards as though they anticipated an ambush. Once they almost turned back, one man grabbing at the sleeve of the other, cursing him in low tones, the boy (?) cowering as though he expected to be struck. But they still came on, more wary and suspicious than ever.

Cries of fear as Jock Houliston suddenly straightened up, a truncheon clasped in his hand.

"You're under arrest, all three of you." A pair of handcuffs were dangled ostentatiously. "Now, James Foster, let's be having you. You're all going to accompany me to the police station where . . ."

Houliston's jubilant caution died away as he saw their

faces for the first time, tried to match that police photo of Foster with one of them. *Oh Christ Almighty, those hideous countenances belonged anywhere except in a civilized twentieth-century society, pockmarked scarred faces that even the mist failed miserably to hide.* Wretched beings that cringed and whined, the boy on his knees covering his head with his hands as though he expected a blow. Ragged clothing torn in many places so that the flesh was visible beneath, skin that was a mass of blackheads, an unwashed poverty-stricken trio, their bare feet bleeding where they had scratched them on the stones.

"Have mercy on us, sir," the taller of the two men cried. "Take our boat, our cargo, but let us go, I beg of you for we only do this else we starve, and the Lord alone knows we are close to that now."

Jock Houliston grunted. Certainly they spoke the truth but what the hell was going on? Bitter disappointment because none of these was the man he wanted, that much was clear. He found himself backing away a step, revolted at that which confronted him. *An explanation, oh just give me a logical explanation for all this.*

"What's going on?" he grunted.

They stared back at him in amazement, did not reply.

"Come on, I'm a police officer and I want to know what's going on!"

"You . . . don't know?" The tall man seemed to be their spokesman, one who trembled visibly, slobbered as he spoke. *"Police?* What's that? You're not Customs men, or is this a devilish trick?"

Houliston jangled the handcuffs, saw how they started, huddled together in sheer terror like sheep in a slaughterhouse smelling death.

"No, sir, not the dungeons, we beg you. Kill us, but not that!"

"You're stark raving bloody barmy," the policeman muttered, and thought to himself "and so am I." Still holding the handcuffs he unclipped his radio, flicked a button. "One-seven-one-five, come in please."

There should have been an instant crackling, a voice answering him. There was nothing. With a chill of fear trickling up his back he realized that for some reason his radio was dead. No reason, just a lifeless object that could neither give nor receive messages; his link with civilization was broken. He was on his own.

"Please, *sur,* take our boat, our cargo . . ."

I don't want your bloody boat or your cargo. I want James Foster and four other missing people. "Look, let's start at the beginning, just tell me who you are and what you're doing here."

Silence. Blank, terror-stricken stares, the boy starting to sob. He couldn't have been more than ten, Houliston thought. He'd been ill-treated, starved, should be taken into care. The police officer's flesh was prickling. He didn't want to be the one to do that, didn't want to have to *touch* any of them and he'd handled some pretty revolting corpses in his time. Like old Matthews, the hermit who had lived in that old pillbox down by the canal. He'd died one hot summer and hadn't been missed for almost a month. When Houliston found him the wasps had made quite a sizable nest inside him. But rather that than *this!*

Maybe I could just leave them here, catch up with the others. I don't even have to say I've seen them, do I?

It was the boy who screamed, a piercing yell of soul-shattering terror, pointing into the mist behind Jock Houliston. Grunts and cries from the other two. "They're here, we knew they were somewhere about . . ."

"It's the search party." Houliston wheeled round, almost screamed himself, tried to shout "I'm a police officer, d'you hear me," but no words would come.

Shapes loomed out of the mist, figures that bore a faint resemblance to the human body until you saw their faces. Long coats, triangular hats pulled well down as though even they tried to spare you from looking upon their features. Grotesque, evil. Menacing; wielding clubs and pistols.

"Tak' them," they chorused—a cry that embodied hate and sadistic lust, a tone that surely no human vocal cords could have issued.

There must have been a dozen of them, perhaps more, running, shouting. A pistol boomed, its cloud of villainous sulfurous smoke turning the swirling mist yellow, giving off acrid fumes. Converging on the two men and the boy, vicious blows from raised cudgels splitting open the latter's head; you heard them, *felt* them. They were battering his skull into a mulch, *but there was not a spot of blood to be seen!* Seizing his companions; then turning to face this stranger who had no business skulking in the fog of a smugglers' marsh.

"Another 'un!" One of them grunted his surprise. "Tak' 'un, too."

Shocked awareness flooded Jock Houliston's numbed brain. His common sense rebelled, demanded logic where there was none. I'm a policeman and I'm not standing for this. Twenty-five years of training, taught to cope with a thousand and one different situations, even if this one didn't slot into any particular niche. His instinct surfaced, defied surrealism; that time there had been a fancy-dress party and the guests had got drunk, run amok. It was like that now. He had arrested four of them single-handed then, locked them in the cells for the night to sober up.

He drove forward with his truncheon, a stabbing blow in the manner of a dueling swordsman, finding his target, the nearest man's solar plexus. It should have doubled his assailant up, had him writhing on the ground, clutching at his stomach. It didn't.

The blow jarred Jock Houliston's arm right up to his shoulder, had him almost dropping his weapon. The other seemed unaware that he had been struck, came on unhindered, strong cold fingers encircling the constable's throat. Squeezing, throttling. And more of them were coming in on the fray, sheer weight of numbers bearing him to the ground.

Jock Houliston fought in blind fear, swung his truncheon again but it was wrested from his grip, his arms pinioned behind him. Kicking, bone-jarring, toe-breaking blows that found their mark but brought not so much as a gasp of pain from his attackers. His legs were seized, his body lifted up.

"To the dungeons?" Someone asked the question in a lisping hollow voice.

"Nae." There followed a pause as though the one to whom the question had been directed was thinking, forced to make an instant decision. "There's things happenin' at the Castle, we'd better keep clear. Nae, ta the bog, 'tis quickest!"

Houliston was aware of being carried, borne over rough ground, jerked and shaken, his stomach threatening to erupt. His trained mind again; you're a policeman, they're assaulting you. The wood and the marsh is teeming with police, you'll be rescued any second.

But nobody came to his rescue. Wherever the search party had gone they were oblivious of his fate, a land of mist and silence, the only sound the steady tramping of feet across soggy terrain. Houliston closed his eyes. It was a nightmare and when he awoke it would be gone, just a few faint awful memories. Catnapping on his bed in between double shifts, in the morning they were going to scour Droy Wood. It had played on his mind.

His captors had stopped and the fingers that gripped him bit deep into his flesh, burned him with their cold. Lifting him again, above their heads into the fog, thick grayness everywhere.

He knew only too well what they were about to do, smelled the foul gases of some nearby bog. One last time he tried to struggle and gave up because they had him imprisoned at full stretch with their unbelievable strength. A shout, more of a whispered croak. "I'm a police officer and you're under arrest."

Next came a sudden sensation of freedom, a release from those bony manacles, a wave of vertigo as he was catapulted into the air. Going up, flailing the air with arms and legs, slowing as he reached his apex. Starting to fall, a kind of headlong dive, instinctively taking a breath and holding it. And then he hit the bog.

A splash as though the water had solidified, wallowing up to his thighs in slimy stinking mud. Struggling, sinking in another foot. Up to his waist now, floundering and trying not to panic. More than just a bog, quicksands with shallow-rooted rushes cunningly disguising it so that an unwary traveler might stumble into it. Nature's own death trap.

The mist had eddied and for a few brief moments PC Jock Houliston saw his attackers again, ringed around the edge of the bog, their hideous faces masked by the shadows cast by their wide headgear. He could not see their expressions yet he felt their malevolence, a blast of sheer cold hate.

Why, oh Jesus Christ, *why* are you doing this to me?

He sank in another few inches; it was too late to try and extricate himself by lying full length, he had gone in too deep. The mud stirred noisily, greedily, devouring him by the second, pulling him down avidly.

"Just bloody well tell me *why!*"

No answer. These creatures who roamed the mists of Droy Wood and its marshes answered to nobody for their actions. The laws were of their own making, since the days when they had been commanded to apprehend those who came ashore secretly, and they saw no reason to change anything.

The policeman had resigned himself to death, did not even attempt to prolong his life when his chin slipped below the shifting mud. It was dark, night already, he had been in this bog for hours; it had seemed only minutes.

And somewhere, not too far away, he could hear men shouting, dogs barking excitedly as they picked up a scent. One last flicker of hope had him opening his mouth, mustering his breath for a final scream that would bring the search party in this direction.

He almost made it, but his cry for help was drowned by a rush of foul liquid mud pouring into his open mouth.

THIRTEEN

Andy Dark hauled himself up into the lower branches of the towering oak tree, pulled Carol up behind him. Climbing, helping her from one bough up onto the next, and all the time Bertie Hass was still shooting. The shots vibrated the damp night air, then died away to a frantic metallic clicking.

A snarling and growling, an animal yelping with pain somewhere.

"They're wolves, all right," Andy muttered. "They can't be anything else."

"It's impossible." Carol closed her eyes, tried to convince herself that at any second she would wake up. Please God let it all be a nightmare, a fever brought on by stubbornly walking home in the pouring rain the other night. She hadn't been picked up and raped by a stranger, not imprisoned in those terrible dungeons. The German didn't exist, she wasn't clinging to a branch of a tree, scared she might fall, with ravenous wolves down below. Because wolves were long gone from Britain.

The wolves were baying more persistently now. If you peered into the gloom you could just make out flitting shadowy shapes that might have been Alsatian dogs. Only you knew they weren't.

"Something's gone terribly wrong," Andy said.

"What do you mean?"

"It's like the whole wood has come to life. Not just a crackpot German who's still fighting World War II. Time hasn't just slipped back forty years, it's reverted centuries, maybe even further, got sort of all mixed up. Like it's been waiting for thousands of years for something to happen and now it's all happening at once. A kind of spoof film only you're bang in the middle of it and it's all for real."

"What are we going to do?"

"For the moment we can't do anything except stop right here."

Waiting and listening, knowing that it wasn't a fevered dream, praying for it to get light. For the mist to clear; for a party of searchers to appear armed with guns. Clutching at vain hopes, knowing in their hearts that they were all going to come to nothing.

"I can't understand why somebody hasn't come looking for us," Carol said. "Surely they've found the Mini and your Land Rover. They must know we're in here so why don't they come?"

"They probably have," he replied. "But I guess . . . the wood isn't the same for everybody. Maybe all they see is fog and a dense wood that they have to rely on the dogs to search. I don't know, it defies explanation. I'm only guessing anyway."

Seconds later they heard the German screaming, hoarse cries of fear, a renewed snarling; it sounded like the wolves were fighting among themselves. It lasted perhaps a minute, no longer, and then the silence rolled back.

"How horrible." Carol Embleton was trying not to conjure up a picture in her mind of a strange uniformed man being torn apart by savage beasts that should have been extinct for centuries.

"He didn't make it up into the trees," Andy said quietly, slipping a reassuring arm around Carol. "Time had run out for him. I reckon that parachutist coming down out of the sky tonight was his death sign. Poor sod, but he wasn't . . . *real,* to explain it simply. I guess he didn't *feel* anything. I can't explain it any other way."

They lapsed into silence, reluctant to put their thoughts into words. It would have to get light eventually; at least they hoped it would. There was no guarantee. Droy Wood defied not just the laws of Nature but those of the universe as well.

"What's that?" Carol must have dozed, awoke with a start, aware of a numbness in her legs, cramped so that she might have fallen if Andy had not been supporting her. She heard a distant rushing sound like a series of waterfalls in full spate, recalled a childhood visit to the Elan Valley where she had stared in awe at the mighty foaming dams.

"It's the sea," Andy Dark replied. "I know for a fact that this week there are the highest tides of the year. Sometimes, according to the locals, the wood has been flooded right up to the road." The road, oh what wouldn't we give just to set foot on that hard flat tarmac. "I've never witnessed the autumn tides myself and you can't always believe what the villagers tell you, but that sea sounds bloody angry to me. I'd've thought there would have been a raging gale in that case, one to blow this damned fog away. Hey, it's starting to get light!"

The fog was turning a lighter shade of gray, they could make out the shapes of the trees around them, boles that became faces again. Expressions. If you stared at them long enough you read something that transcended malevolence. Fear! It was as though Droy Wood itself was afraid, engendering an atmosphere of impending doom, hell awaiting its own collapse.

The light was coming fast, the vapor now taking on a faint rosy hue as though the sun were trying to break through, a battle of the elements with a raging sea providing eerie background music. But still there was no wind, just a deadly unnatural calm.

Andy tensed, thought he heard a scream somewhere but he could not be sure. A single yell of pain and terror like Bertie Hass had made when the wolves bunched and rushed him.

"Well, we can't stay here." The conservation officer finally put into words his thoughts of the past half hour.

"We're not . . . going down *there!*" Carol gripped his arm. "We can't, Andy. The wolves . . . !"

"The wolves have gone." At least I bloody well hope so. "I don't think we'll have any more trouble from them but if we hear them we'll just have to shin up the nearest tree. If we stay up here much longer we'll get so cramped we'll fall anyway."

"I suppose you're right." She was staring into the mist, making out shapes that could have been wolves but probably were not. In this wood anything might be just anything, or, on the other hand, nothing at all. You never found out until it was too late.

"I've been thinking," she wasn't going to like this very much, "if we just go on blindly like this we'll end up even more lost than we already are."

"So?"

"Our best plan is to head back to Droy House."

"No!" Carol pulled away from him. "Anywhere but *there.* You're mad."

"Just listen, will you?" Andy grabbed her wrist, thought for a moment that she was going to make a run for it. "There's a flat roof to the house," unless it's bloody well altered shape again, "and if we could find a way up there we'd be above the level of the treetops."

"It might just clear"—a vain hope—"but I reckon we could probably attract attention from there. They've *got* to be searching the wood by now. We can holler, scream, make one helluva din."

Carol bit her lip, shuddered visibly. What Andy said made sense. The German was gone but those awful dungeons were still there. "All right, I guess we've got nothing to lose now."

The moment they reached the ground their legs buckled under them, the numbness beginning to tingle, discomfort escalating into pain. Sheer agony, rubbing at their limbs in an attempt to speed up the circulation. And then shakily they were retracing their steps down that muddy water-logged track, their feet sinking in at every step.

"There's a lot of water lying," Andy muttered, "more than there was last night . . . as though the sea is steadily creeping into the wood." He had to shout now to make himself heard above the pounding of waves. "I think the tide's going to cover the wood!" A disconcerting thought, remembering that time when he had gone out with the coast-guard because a man gathering mussels had been trapped on the mudflats, a wide creek filling up between him and the shore, cutting off his retreat. They had just been in time. Now they had another reason for returning to Droy House, an island in the midst of the flooding; being *driven* there.

"Look!" Carol stopped, pointed. Ahead of them on the path lay a mud-covered pistol, one that they both recognized instantly. Bertie Hass's Luger. Beside it was the holster belt and leather ammunition pouch. Nothing else;

no body, no remnants of a Luftwaffe uniform torn to shreds by vicious fangs.

"It's the German's all right." Andy picked it up, examined it, ejected the spent shells, smelled burned cordite. "And at least it's real enough. I wonder . . ."

He lifted up the belt, unclipped the flap of the pouch, poured the shiny brass cartridges into his hand. Live ones, as good as the day they left the factory.

He loaded the weapon, dropped the belt back onto the ground and put the spare cartridges in his pocket. "Well, at least we're armed." He tried to sound confident for Carol's benefit. There certainly weren't any dead wolves lying around, not even a trace of blood. Not that he expected to find any.

"Come on," he said, pushing on ahead, "the sooner we get back to the house, the better. There's water seeping up everywhere, this place is getting like a bath sponge." He was concerned, had that awful feeling that they were never going to get out of the wood.

Once the sunlight broke through the fog but the vapor instantly closed in, shut it out again. Droy Wood was fighting desperately to preserve its evil secrets, determined that those who entered should not leave.

Andy peered ahead. The house could not be far away now. He experienced a sinking feeling; suppose the powers that controlled this domain of evil had snatched it away as they had removed the German. Here, anything was possible. His mouth was dry and if the path had not been a veritable quagmire he would have broken into a run.

There was something on the track ahead of them. At first he thought it was a sapling and then it moved, stepped out to bar their way. Instinctively the Luger came up, his finger resting on the trigger. It was a human being, a female, even in the dim outline in the fog, sensuous, naked like Carol Embleton had been.

"Thelma!" Carol gave a cry, but even then she could not be sure, the wisps of gray mist almost obliterating the features although it could not destroy the overall picture of a girl she had grown up with. Her instinct was to rush forward but for some reason she held back. Something wasn't quite right . . .

Ten yards separated them, it might as well have been a hundred. Thelma Brown's eyes flickered behind the opaqueness, a dim torch-bulb that was faulty, threatening to go out.

"Do not go on." Her voice was a scarcely audible whisper as though it required a tremendous effort to speak; hoarse and straining, trying to say more but the words would not come. "Go back . . . go back . . . go back . . ." The mist thickened, covered her, and when it swirled again she was gone.

"Where is she?" Carol Embleton asked in a hushed whisper.

But Andy Dark was not listening; he was running forward, plowing his way through mud and pools of water that splashed up, saturating his already damp trousers. He did not expect to catch a glimpse of Thelma, no more than he had expected to find the body of Bertie Hass lying back there where the wolves had ravaged him. He stooped down, examined the ground, saw the remnants of their own footmarks from the previous night, his own crisscrossed Wellington imprints, Carol's bare feet. But neither the German's nor Thelma Brown's!

"Why did she run away?" Carol sensed the stupidity of her own question, half guessed the answer that hammered in her brain. *Because she's already dead like the others here. And they snatched her away because she tried to warn us.*

"It was some kind of hallucination." Andy could not think of a better reply on the spur of the moment. "It wasn't really her at all." Not a deliberate lie, just a guess.

"She warned us," Carol whispered. "We can't go back to the house."

"Then where else are we going to go, you tell me?"

"I . . . I don't know."

"And neither do I. We can't stop out here another night. I doubt if the house is any more dangerous than the wood. And, anyway, they should be looking for us soon. If we can only let them know where we are."

They walked on in silence. The sunlight seemed to have given up its battle with the Droy fog; it was impossible to judge what time of day it was but surely it was still morning. It could not be more than an hour since daylight had broken.

They came upon the house suddenly, a huge turreted shape rearing up out of the gloom, frowning down on them. *Go back, go back.* Carol heard Thelma's warning again, would have turned and run had not Andy been holding her. A token resistance but where he went, she would go.

The hall looked exactly the same as it had when they had left it a few hours ago, that same stench of decay, the paneling rotting with age, the trap door in the far corner. She didn't want to look at it, didn't dare guess what lay in the dungeons below, elevated her eyes to the crumbling stairway. It looked dangerous in places, entire steps missing, as though it would collapse if anyone put their full weight upon it.

Andy walked toward the stairs, noticed that the floor was wet, small puddles lying on the uneven surface.

Somewhere water was trickling; the dungeons, they were flooded. He could hear the water lapping below the trap door. Soon it would push upward and lift the hatch.

His foot was on the bottom step, Carol close behind him, when something made him glance up. The landing was in shadow, a dark damp platform with half the balustrade missing. Something moved, came forward and for one terrible second Carol thought that it was Thelma again, but the silhouette was wrong, too bulky. A man.

Now they could see him clearly, the silken clothes which had once been the finery of gentry, the waistcoat straining on the protruding stomach, the jowled scowling features, thinning long gray hair. Eyes that flicked and pierced the watchers like rapiers, thick lips curling into a sneer. The spider viewed the flies in its web with loathsome gloating.

"I was expecting you." Nasal tones, wheezing as though even speech required a considerable effort. "Let us go and view the Droy lands for the last time, for now the sea, which had been kept back for thousands of years, has come to reclaim its own." He laughed, a hollow chuckle that echoed across the empty hall. "A few more hours and the lands of my forefathers will have gone forever. Yet it is a fitting end." A sigh that embodied deep sadness. "Far rather that than that it should be wrested from us by usurpers to the title."

Andy Dark stared up at the man on the landing, felt a fleeting humility as a serf might have experienced centuries before when summoned before his master, wilted beneath the gaze from those deepset small eyes. One who juggled with the fate of others.

"The police are coming." It sounded trite, a last desperate throw, your final card when muggers cornered you in an ill-lit subway. Remembering the loaded Luger in his hand; token bravado, just a gesture of defiance. "They'll pull this place apart."

"They'll be too late, the sea will do it for them. For years Droy Wood had been eroded, the water creeping in, until it was virtually floating. A waterlogged sailing ship that is ready to be submerged. Everything will be lost forever without trace," the other gave another forced laugh, "and maybe then none of us will be forced to live on any longer. Come though, we are wasting time. Let us go aloft and bid the Droy lands farewell ere we go down with them."

Andy felt his feet beginning to move, mounting the steps slowly, heard Carol following. The stairs seemed firm and strong. Perhaps they had recently been renovated and the repairs were not visible. Oak paneling that no longer bore the pockmarks of woodworm. Shadowy, so that the figure at the top of the stairs was a silhouette again, his arrogant features fading back into the darkness.

There was a roaring in Andy Dark's ears; it could have been the distant angry sea. A stench that reminded him of rotting seaweed. He lurched, clutched at the stair rail to steady himself, his stomach rolling as it might have done on board a ship floundering in tempestuous seas; the captain up there on the bridge. We're sinking, we're all going down with the ship. Let's drown with dignity, not panicking like bilge rats.

Going on up, the man at the top turning as if to lead the way, his ungainly bulk moving surprisingly gracefully.

"Andy," said Carol in a frightened whisper, "we shouldn't have come here, we should have heeded Thelma's warning."

Now they were standing on a stone balcony that jutted

out at the back of the big house which had once been a castle, floating in a white swirling mist.

And somewhere far down below they heard the lapping and splashing of water.

FOURTEEN

Muffin was back close at Roy Bean's heels, so close that at times she threatened to obstruct his difficult progress through the swampy ground. Angrily he kicked back at her, heard her whimper but she did not move away, just cringed.

"Stupid bitch," he grunted. "You're supposed to be working the rough, searching for a scent like those bloody police dogs are." Strangely, the Alsatians had gone quiet. Perhaps they were trained to work silently. Or else they were acting strangely, too.

Hell, this fog was thicker than ever and yet you could hear the sea pounding the coastline as it hadn't done since that disastrous week of the Fastnet yacht race some years ago. It was crazy, a raging sea but here in Droy Wood you experienced the kind of feeling old-time mariners must have had when they were becalmed. The wind's never going to blow again, you're here for the rest of your life and there isn't much of that left now.

The gamekeeper struggled in a patch of soft ground, the thick springy grass beneath his feet giving him the impression that it was floating on water, that at any second it might tip up and throw him into a deep pool. Muffin was wallowing, almost swimming, snorting the way she always did when she retrieved a shot bird off the water. It hadn't been as wet as this the other day. Christ, it was always swampy in here but this was ridiculous, frightening if you thought too much about it.

No longer was it easy to keep the men directly on either side of you in sight. Not just because the mist was appreciably thicker but now they were in the densest part of the wood where they were forced to detour impassable barriers such as bogs and impenetrable patches of brambles. Even if the syndicate demanded to shoot the wood the beaters wouldn't stand for it, Roy Bean reflected. And neither would I. I never want to set foot in this fucking place again.

He had given up urging the spaniel forward. She had a stubborn streak in her and she'd made up her mind not to range from her master's side. Any other time, anywhere else, she would have had a thrashing. Bloody dog!

He paused for a moment. Perhaps he wasn't as fit as he thought, he rarely got out of breath. The stink in here didn't help, a mixture of decaying trees, marsh vapors and rotting seaweed drifting in from the sea. He glanced about him; there was nobody in sight at this very moment, he could not even hear the other searchers splashing and cursing. It gave you a funny feeling like suddenly everybody else had left and you were abandoned here, hadn't a clue which way to go. Once you lost your sense of direction in thick fog you didn't find it again unless by chance you stumbled upon a recognizable landmark. And here in the wood everywhere looked the same, every stunted tree like the next one. But at least today you could hear the sea, knew that if it was on the left then the road had to be on your right. Well, at least it *should* be. He shuddered.

Roy Bean set off again, an urgency about his movements now, a disregard for the water that slopped over the tops of his Wellington boots. He should have worn waders but how the hell were you to know that the fucking place was going to flood?

Muffin stopped, cowered and whined. Oh Jesus Christ, not only are you refusing to work but now you bleedin' well don't want to do anything! He lifted his ash stick threateningly and at that moment the spaniel gave a short sharp bark, the way she warned him when there was a trespasser somewhere close by on the game preserves; except that now it was a yelp of fear, ears flat back on her liver and white head, tail curled down between her hind legs.

He was about to strike her when a movement distracted him, an eddying of the fog up ahead of him, revealing an outline then closing back over it again. One of the searchers must have gone too far, realized his mistake and come back, was trying to locate the line again. Silly bugger, if you were beating for me on shooting days you'd get a cursing. That's how beaters get shot, buggering about all over the place.

"Oi!" Roy's shout was strangely subdued, muffled. "Over here, mate."

The fog rolled away from the other once more, and as it swirled the spaniel gave another bark, jumped and ran in the opposite direction, splashing, swimming; fleeing in sheer canine terror.

But Roy Bean scarcely noticed the departure of his dog as he was afforded a clear view of the man ahead of him, aware that the other man was stark naked, that the features were familiar, identical with those plastered on walls and telegraph poles all over the village. Instant recognition, mind-blowing shock. Oh my God, it's *him*. *Foster!* Hundreds of bloody searchers and it has to be *me* who finds him. Not wanting to believe his eyes. It was some trick of the mist or his imagination playing him up.

Bean shouted again. "Oi, the bugger's here. Oi, you lot, where the fuck are you?"

His words seemed to bounce off the wall of fog at him. That sea was making so much noise that nobody could hear him. *If only they'd let me bring the gun but all I've got is a bloody stick.*

James Foster was smiling. There was something wrong with his throat, as if it had been cut, only it couldn't have been or else he wouldn't be standing there now. *The bugger's only dangerous to women. What's happened to that nature conservancy bloke and the decoy copper then?*

Foster turned, began to walk slowly into the mist.

"Oi." The gamekeeper began to move after him. "Oi, you. There's hundreds of police here. You're surrounded, you can't get away."

The other did not appear to have heard him, indeed he might even have forgotten that there was anybody there. Sauntering away, almost casually, Roy Bean struggling to keep him in sight. Any moment the mist would billow over and he would be gone. *I couldn't 'elp it, sir. I shouted but nobody came. Tried to follow 'im but I couldn't keep up with 'im, lost 'im in the bleedin' fog.*

But you are keeping up with him. Better not actually catch him up. Any second somebody will come and then we'll have the bastard. Come on you bloody lot, where are you?

There wasn't anybody else; just Roy Bean and James Foster in the middle of a wood that was getting more swampy with every step they took. "Oi, you!"

Floundering, trying to keep Foster in sight, not because he wanted to apprehend him but because there wasn't anybody else here. Just the two of them in a world where nobody else had ever existed and Man was a gregarious species.

Bean's chest was beginning to hurt, a constricting pain that spread right down and burned like a stitch in his side. Ahead of him the naked man slowed, a dim outline only just visible in this vile fog, as though he deliberately hung back so that his pursuer would not lose sight of him. A hand was raised in mocking gesture. Hurry, time is running out; for both of us.

The gamekeeper had lost a Wellington boot, had had to abandon it in the mud as he struggled free. I want to go back. Which way is back? Where is everybody else? Trying to shout but if he did manage it then it was drowned by the roaring in his own ears.

The stench was stronger now, burning the back of his throat, making him throw up but he could not afford to delay, vomiting as he fought his way through a thick reed-bed, cascading the remnants of his breakfast down the front of his shirt. Stuck again, having to leave his remaining rubber boot somewhere down in . . . *there*! *He recoiled, spewed again. That mud, it was of a texture that he had never seen before, sloppy gray slime that bubbled and hissed, reminding him of slugs when you trod on them, how they burst into a filthy mess so that your foot skidded.* It was oozing up out of the reeds, streaking the black water, covering it. Mother of God, it was as though the effluent of Mankind since the dawn of civilization were being rejected by Earth, thrown back up. Take your vile pollution back! Everywhere was awash with it.

A pit of some kind on his left, filling steadily with this bubbling slime and . . . *there was somebody in it, an unrecognizable figure attempting to swim, mouthing screams in one continual vomit of the stuff.* Man or woman, it was impossible to tell, perhaps not even human, a despairing arm raised and then it was gone, just a mass of bubbles marking its demise. And then they burst and you tried to convince yourself that it was a hallucination, a despicable trick of the brain in this awful dead place. You could imagine anything here.

Foster was no longer to be seen. The gamekeeper glanced about him. No, don't go and leave me here. I don't want to harm you, I hope you escape. Show me the way out of here and I'll swear on the Bible that I never even saw you.

Everywhere the mud was oozing and thickening, hissing its hate for those who ventured into this place where they had no right to be. Movements everywhere, flitting shapes that might just have been created by the eddying fog. Figures that came and went before you could be sure, afraid to call out to them in case they were . . . you dared not think what they might be. Malevolent whisperings, rising to a crescendo, dying away, beginning again. And all the time you were fighting a battle to stop yourself from being sucked down—like that figure in the pit!

Roy clutched at a branch but it snapped off, showered him with splinters of damp rotted wood. He grabbed at another and it held. Just. He tried to think logically. The sea was responsible for all this . . . For centuries it had been creeping into Droy Wood, reclaiming the territory that had once been its own, filling gutters and making pools, a slow process that had now come to fruition. And then the marsh gave off its gases, created the fog. So you got lost and . . .

He started, recoiled so that the branch broke and threw him back against the trunk. There was a man standing only a few yards away, enshrouded in the mist so that his features were obscured but Roy Bean knew that it wasn't Foster. The shape was wrong and the other was wearing some kind of heavy uniform, a kind of soft helmet on his head. He must have been there all the time, just watching, waiting.

"Who . . . are you?" The gamekeeper didn't know if he actually managed to get the words out.

"Too late." The other spoke with a guttural accent, slowly as though the language were unfamiliar to him and he had to dwell on each word. "I have waited patiently all these years in vain."

"What are you talking about?"

"Just as the Russian winter defeated us so the elements have again risen to help the enemy. The mist has shrouded and hidden this place, the bogs made an invasion impossible. Elsewhere the German army had triumphed. Except here. Only I represent the Fatherland here and I will defend it to the last." Bertie Hass spoke grimly, his fingers feeling for a holster belt that was no longer around his waist.

You're mad, Bean thought, swallowed and felt slime slithering down the back of his throat. This couldn't be happening, it was all in the mind like that guy being sucked down in that deep bog. Or else it was somebody playing a bloody stupid trick.

"The war's over," he said. "A long time ago."

"You lie, just as the others did, a trick to lure me from my stronghold. This wood shall not be surrendered. Consider yourself my prisoner, a prisoner of war."

"I . . . look . . . the searchers can't be far away," he stammered, looking blindly about him for somewhere to flee but there was nowhere, just mud that was becoming more liquid by the second.

"Hurry, we have no time to waste!"

Roy Bean did not want to go, was resisting every movement his limbs made against his will, feet squelching in and out of the foul stinking morass that could no longer be termed mud, aware that somehow this man who claimed to be a Nazi was driving him on. Through the murk, along waterlogged footpaths, zigzagging and unerringly finding and following one track after another. Not talking because there was nothing to talk about, aware of the other's presence right behind him, hearing again those words "Hurry, we have no time to waste."

A huge shape loomed up before them, a turreted building that might have been a medieval castle, sinister in the gloom as though it had been deliberately lurking there waiting for them. You felt its coldness, its hate, a monster that was dying a lingering death and sought to vent its malevolence on somebody before it was too late. Those windows seemed to gleam for a second or two as if a shaft of wan sunlight had broken through the fog. But that was impossible, the sun would never shine here again.

It *has* to be Droy House, Roy Bean tried to convince himself. But so much older, the way it might have looked once. Frightening, a sadistic illustrator of children's books inflicting subtle horror on his readers; they wanted to slam the book shut, throw it away, but instead they were forced to stare at it, and during the nocturnal hours it would return to haunt their dreams, so much more real.

Perhaps the German pushed him, Roy Bean could not be sure. He stumbled forward, felt stonework beneath his feet, solid steps that were treacherous with a coating of slime, harbor steps with a polluted tide lapping at them.

The bare walls of the hallway streamed with foul condensation, the floor slippery. An open trap door in the far corner; he wanted to back away, to flee outside, but something held him there, drew him toward it. He tried to scream but no sound came from his lips, clutching at the wall as he descended the uneven steps into the cold blackness below. *This can't be happening!* It is.

Icy water, thick with slime, came up to his ankles. This underground place was flooding, we'll be drowned. Yet his protests were mute, his movements jerky. Don't touch me, please, I'll do as you say.

Pinioned against the wall, something hard snapped on his wrists and ankles; hanging there. He didn't know whether his captor was still here or not, just listening to the smooth swilling of thick liquid. The dungeon was filling up, like melting slush, mentally measuring its progress as it crept up his body, obscenely exploring inside his saturated clothing; numbing him.

Voices, indistinguishable whispers, people moving about but seemingly unaware of his presence, trying to call out to them but his vocal cords had long ceased to function.

The scum lapped at his navel, submerged it.

Somebody was weeping somewhere, it sounded like a girl or a young boy, he could not be sure which, sobs which eventually died away. And then he saw the dual red pinpoints of dozens of pairs of eyes, knew that they belonged to rodents. Rats, swimming, trying to escape but in the end they would drown too.

Suddenly one bit him, sharp teeth gouging his thigh, and he writhed to the full extent of his manacles, jerked and strained, instinctively tried to pull away. They were all coming at him now; he could only see their eyes but he knew only too well what the repulsive bodies looked like, brown furry creatures that scavenged, lived on filth, and attacked helpless humans. Just one rat bite was capable of . . . God, he knew only too well what dangers rats presented . . . On the game preserves they were one of his main enemies. They ate eggs, young chicks, bit their way into feed bags and spoiled what they didn't eat. Left their turds everywhere and even when you poisoned them they managed to crawl into their holes beneath the out-buildings and you had to live with the stench of decomposing rats for weeks during the summer.

Just one rat bite could . . . his skin crawled and he sensed that thigh wound bleeding, tinging the slime pink.

Ratbite fever, the wound would fill with fluid; it already was, with contaminated sludge.

Or Weil's disease.

Or ringworm. Or . . .

But he wouldn't get any of those because he would drown first. Christ, he hated rats. In the past he had killed thousands of them; poison, traps, an air rifle on the banks of the stream when he had half an hour to spare. Shooting rats gave him more pleasure than killing any other creature because he despised the little fuckers. You heard the soft "phut" of the pellet as it struck the hairy body, sent it kicking and writhing into the current, turning the water crimson. Looking up at you and you read the agony in its eyes. Die you bastard and don't be too quick about it because I want you to suffer.

Now the tables were turned, the rats had *him* in the water at their mercy. We know you, Roy Bean, what you've been doing to us for years and now it's our turn. *You're* the one who's going to suffer this time. We're all going to drown but not just yet. Not until . . .

They were ripping his clothes below the surface, gripping the material with their teeth, pulling until they tore it into shreds, bared his flesh. No, not *there!*

He tried to close his thighs but the leg irons prevented him. Rough hairy bodies rubbed against his skin and suddenly he was able to scream again. Yells of sheer pain and terror as needlelike teeth found their mark, shooting the agony right up into his stomach, knotting it. He was spewing again, throwing up the filth that he had swallowed, helpless to throw off his attackers as they began their feast of living human flesh, chewing on the tenderest portions first.

Once Roy Bean almost fainted but even that was denied him. The stinking muddy water was up to his chest now and the rats were running up his chest and onto his shoulders, nipping at his neck, squatting there, gloating. Time had stopped, only the agony went on.

He cricked his neck as he strained to keep his head above the level of the rising floodwater; the end would not be long now. The rats were all climbing up on him, almost smothering him with their wet coarse fur as they jostled for places, began to fight among themselves.

He couldn't keep the liquid filth out of his mouth much longer, felt its sliminess against his lips, tried to spit it out. It was slipping down his throat, a sensation like melting ice cream that was contaminated. Coughing, spewing.

And only at the very end did the rats go for his jugular vein.

FIFTEEN

Detective-Sergeant Jim Fillery was becoming increasingly aware that they were going to have to abandon the search before very long. He cursed, took it as a personal affront by the elements. They had combined to thwart him, evil hiding evil. Foster was in here, all right, he knew it. Hunches were an experienced policeman's finest asset; when you were a rookie you were inclined to jump to conclusions, but after a few years you sorted out the possibilities and got a feeling for them. Which was why Jim Fillery knew that Foster had not left Droy Wood.

The ground was flooding fast. Somewhere the tide was flowing in, might even reach as far up as the road. The mist was thickening, too, rising up out of the boggy ground in typical autumnal style except that now it did so with a vengeance.

Men to his right and left were floundering, having to make detours, leaving large patches of thick reeds untouched. It was destroying any scent which the dogs might have picked up, too. In all, a bloody waste of time. Except for that nagging hunch; keep going, you're on the right track.

Nevertheless, the search would have to be called off soon, the detective could not avoid that. If anybody got drowned or lost the media would flay the police; there were times when you couldn't win and this was one of them.

And then he saw the house, a tumbledown ruin that

the swamp was going to destroy, the clearing waterlogged with this stinking slime. Jim Fillery got his hunch again, more positive than before, almost like the scent the dogs were supposedly searching for, a fox earth which the hounds knew was inhabited.

"I'm going to check the house," he called out to the man on his right who was just visible in the gloom. "Tell the others to form a cordon around it, just in case." His words sounded strangely muffled but the other raised a hand to show that he had understood. Check the house, then we'll call it a day. But we will anyway because the feeling's strong, very strong. Fillery slipped his hand in his pocket, felt the comforting hard metallic coldness of his gun. He would not hesitate to use it if he had to, maybe he would anyway. A policeman was missing, probably dead, and that was one time when emotions ruled.

The door was open a foot or so, hanging by a single rusty hinge. He squeezed through the gap, drew his pistol from his pocket, his keen eyes taking in the hallway. That trap door was closed but thick muddy water was lifting it so that it virtually floated. The cellar was flooded, overflowing. Foster wouldn't be down there. If he was then the State had been spared a lot of expense.

He glanced toward the stairs and that was when he knew, realization hitting him like the backhanders his mother used to lash out with when he was a boy. He saw the footmarks, muddy imprints that were still wet, telling their own story. Heavy crisscross bars of rubber Wellington soles, smaller naked ones following in their wake. A man and a woman.

Fillery's brain was already working on permutations:
(1) PC Lee and Thelma Brown.
(2) James Foster and Carol Embleton.

(3) Andy Dark and . . . ?

His keen brain was instantly processing the information it had been given. One of the girls, certainly, because both had fled naked into Droy Wood. It was impossible at a glance to tell which but at least one of them was still alive (or had been a very short time ago). Lee and Foster had both left their clothes behind in their respective Minis. Fillery pulled a wry face, felt a surge of disappointment. That only left Dark. Unless of course Foster had murdered either or both men, taken Dark's boots. Or the constable had come upon the nature conservation officer's body, helped himself to his footwear.

But the detective was wasting time surmising; there was only one way to find out. He moved forward, gun at the ready. Somebody was upstairs and he was going up after them.

The staircase creaked, threatened to collapse under his weight, boards rotted and missing. A slow ascent, hating himself for the faint glimmering of fear that smoldered in his stomach, threatened to knot his guts into a hard ball. He remembered that time only a few weeks after he had been promoted to the CID. Some crackpot with a grudge against society had held a fourteen-year-old girl hostage in a high-rise block of flats. The guy had a shotgun, had fired at the police down below, threatened to kill himself and the kid if his demands for freedom and a pardon weren't met. The same kind of mentality as Foster, he had a string of convictions for assaulting young children. Time was running out. Fillery and another detective had gone up in the elevator while those down below attempted to distract the maniac's attention.

Fillery had been in the lead, his companion only too happy to follow behind. They had both been scared as hell. Somebody was going to get killed in the next few minutes, it might be all of them. Suddenly you faced death; it was more of a certainty than a probability. You knew also that you had to kill somebody.

Jim Fillery had wanted to vomit, to run back down those stairs, tell the super he wasn't going to die for anybody. But something pushed him forward, transcended his terror. He didn't know what it was, never really found out. But he'd gone on, kicked the door down, and inside that tiny flat the man had just been sitting propped up in the corner. The girl hadn't even gone hysterical and that was when the anticlimax had struck him. In a way it was a letdown because he had never had to push himself past that final barrier, test himself.

Until now. He had to go through it all again.

Along the landing, up on to the second floor. And then he saw the balcony with three people standing on it, a stone ledge that might decide to crumble at any second. His stomach flipped, began to tighten, churning his bowels.

Dark and Carol Embleton. The former was holding a pistol in his hand, dangling at arm's length as though he had forgotten that he had it, the girl clutching his other arm, both of them staring transfixed at the man who faced them.

That was when Fillery's terror threatened to erupt inside him. That bloated jowled face, the flesh resembling that of a fish that was beginning to decompose, eyes receding so that the puffy sockets were closing over them. Lips curled into an expression of hate and gloating, ragged clothing that seemed to rot even as you ran your eye over it, a once colorful apparel that moths and time had shredded.

Everything had stopped, a confrontation that had been frozen like a movie still. The three of them might have been dead, rigor mortis somehow holding them erect against a background of swirling mist and the roaring of an angry sea that sounded a lot closer than it had when Fillery had heard it down below.

He watched them closely, knew that they were alive, that he was witnessing some dreadful final act in a drama that had gone on here for a very long time. Noises; it sounded like distant gunfire, explosions, but it could have been the waves pounding on the shoreline. Shouts, probably from the search party down below but they were gone before you could be sure. And somehow you got the feeling that that repulsive figure out there was the focal point of all this, his bearing that of a master rather than a servant.

And then the actors began to move on their precarious stage, the huge man shuffling toward the stone balustrade, pointing and waving a hand, laughing. Andy Dark turned, watched, seemed to nod.

"The sea is reclaiming Droy Wood," the man shrieked. "See and hear it, the way it swallows up the lands of my forefathers but we shall go with it, all of us who have known it. A fitting end and we shall still have our pride. Our enemies have not taken the wood from us," his shrill tone rising to a crescendo, "for in the end we shall triumph over them."

Fillery's mind flicked back to that day when he had burst into the flat, had primed himself to take human life but had been denied. The barrier he had never had to breach, the anticlimax that had deflected his terror, hauled him back from the brink, left a lot of doubts in his mind. And now he had been pushed to that brink again.

His policeman's training screamed at him to stop, tried to jerk the gunhand back. *You're a police officer, you can't!* I can and I will. I've got to, there isn't any other way.

Firing, his target closer and easier than those life-sized dummies on the practice range, the reports vibrating his whole body. Hearing the heavy slugs finding their mark, cutting into that revolting body with a noise as if ripping into thick soggy cardboard. Tearing, lacerating, mutilating.

The body swayed but did not fall. A mass of gashes, ragged open wounds that should have spouted thick red blood. The eye holes deep craters, the lips torn and twisted into the ultimate in malevolent expressions.

And Jim Fillery knew then that he was at the final barrier, the one that separated bravery from cowardice, sanity from madness. So narrow, he almost screamed and ran but at the last second he stayed and watched, conquered his inner self.

Ross Droy, or whatever this manifestation was, sagged back against the stonework and those terrible wounds began to ooze thick fluid, not scarlet blood but revolting gray slime, sludge that dripped in heavy splodges like cow dung, a substance that had its own life and stank of a putrescence that spanned centuries. Death that lived and spread into pools and gave off vile vapors.

All three of them were fleeing back down those stairs, heedless of the way the structure creaked and shuddered, rotted pieces of woodwork snapping off and splashing down onto the slime-covered floor of the hallway below them. Fog wisped in through the partly open door, seeming to take on malicious shapes, threatened to impede their progress.

"Keep going." It was Andy Dark who was in the lead now, elbowing his way ahead of the detective, dragging

Carol with him. "Don't stop, ignore them, whatever they are."

Whatever they are! He didn't want to think about it. The German, Ross Droy . . . some kind of astral projection that had taken on a solid substance, the evil in this foul marsh mud breathing life into bodies that were long dead. Don't think about it.

"Which way?" Fillery pulled up, glanced about him. A gray frightening moving world hemmed them in, while underfoot the stinking slime swilled and grew deeper, an incoming tide of putrefaction. There was no sign of the men he had instructed to surround the house; he had known deep down they would not be here.

Which way, oh Jesus God which way? We've been trying to get out of this place for days! Andy Dark felt himself starting to panic.

"Look!" Andy pointed to where a rivulet of thick slush was oozing its way into the clearing like a giant slug slithering out of the reed-beds. "This stuff is flowing from the coast, and that means if we head directly in the opposite direction we've got to reach the road. We've got to!" Trying to sound confident for the sake of the others. But at least the foul brackish water was on the move now, propelled by this vile substance that was seeping up out of the ground to cover the wood. Right now he couldn't think of anything else. "Keep going and don't stop for anybody or anything."

A howl, escalating into a baying, dying away as suddenly as it had come, a chilling sound that echoed in their brains.

"That must be the Alsatians, they've found a scent," the detective grunted. Somehow he did not sound convincing.

"It's . . ." Carol checked herself just in time.

"It's the Alsatians," Andy snapped. Except that Alsatians don't bay on a scent. He checked his Luger and suddenly it was a futile encumbrance. Bertie Hass had not managed to stop the wolf pack with it. "Don't take any notice of anything, concentrate on keeping our direction."

Several times they had to make a detour, pools that had previously been shallow enough to splash through were now bubbling morasses of what looked like untreated sewage. Andy's greatest fear was that they might be tempted to take an easier path and double back on themselves. Fearfully he watched the murky gloom ahead, afraid that that turreted house might loom into view again. Welcome back, this is the home of Ross Droy and none shall leave it.

The sea was louder now, almost as though a huge tidal wave were pursuing them, a raging vengeful mass of water determined not to be deprived of its prey. They glanced behind them and then suddenly they felt the wind fanning their faces, an unmistakable cooling freshness laced with a tang of seaweed.

"The wind's getting up," Andy yelled above the noise in an attempt to make himself heard. "That's why we can hear the sea. And look . . . *the mist's thinning*!"

True enough the thick gray vapor was losing its density as it was swirled, lurking gray shapes being blown into nothing more harmful than twisted trees. Branches snapped, splashed and floated in the treacly spreading mire. A shrieking that might have been the wind, a screaming and wailing like that of souls in torment.

"My God!" Jim Fillery gasped, "what the hell's going on?" His features were pale and he still gripped his pistol.

"The elements are battling it out." Andy Dark was reluctant to delay. "The wind and sea versus Droy Wood with its foul mists and polluted mud." The termination of centuries of strife, Nature taking on the forces of evil in a way which none would ever truly understand. The final conflict, a kind of Armageddon.

"The road!" It was Carol Embleton who spotted that unmistakable line of ragged hedgerow beyond the trees less than a hundred yards away. *"It's the road!"*

It was. A straight stretch of B-road surfaced with worn tarmac and sparse chippings. They broke into a run, cursed the mud which made one last effort to suck them back, prayed that that which they saw ahead of them was not a mirage sent to taunt them by the dying spirits of the wood.

People were walking along it, standing talking in groups, mud-splattered bewildered searchers who had been lucky enough to make it back to dry land. Some were still out there. Occasionally, borne on the gale, they heard the barking of a dog, a human cry of anguish. But none was prepared to go back in there.

Gratefully Andy Dark grasped at the stools of the hawthorn hedge, heedless of the spiky thorns, pulled Carol up the bank with him, forced his way through the branches. There was no time to search for a gap, they would not be safe until they were clear of Droy Wood.

"Jesus wept!" Jim Fillery followed them, and only when his feet were on solid tarmac did he turn back to look the way they had come. "Just look at that wood, it's awash, half the trees are floating. This tide'll reach the road."

"It will that," Andy Dark agreed, holding Carol close to him. "The sea's been chipping away at that coastline for centuries and now it's finally broken through. I guess that's the end of Droy Wood . . . and everything in it!"

For a few seconds they stood and watched the final

destruction of the wood, swirling foaming water washing over the foul mud, cleansing it, sweeping away the trees whose shallow roots had been dislodged. The mist was gone, replaced by driving spray. Shapes that were gone before you had a chance to identify them. A ruined house which might or might not have been turreted; it crumbled and fell. Within a few hours it would all be one huge seascape. Nature had fought fiercely . . . and won.

"We'd better go home and get some clothes." Andy smiled wryly at his companions. "A hot bath, something to eat and then sleep the clock round. And after that I guess we'll be plied with questions to which there aren't any answers, eh?"

Jim Fillery nodded. This was one report which he wasn't looking forward to writing. It was going to read like some weird way-out piece of fiction.